Books by Elmore Leonard

ELMORE LEONARD

Blood Money
and other stories

HarperTorch
An Imprint of HarperCollins*Publishers*

This book is a work of fiction. The characters, incidents, and dialogue are drawn from the author's imagination and are not to be construed as real. Any resemblance to actual events or persons, living or dead, is entirely coincidental.

HARPERTORCH
An Imprint of HarperCollins*Publishers*
10 East 53rd Street
New York, New York 10022-5299

Copyright © 2006 by Elmore Leonard, Inc.
The Complete Western Stories of Elmore Leonard copyright © 2004 by Elmore Leonard, Inc.
Map designed by Jane S. Kim
Collection editor, Gregg Sutter
ISBN-13: 978-0-06-112163-0
ISBN-10: 0-06-112163-0

First HarperTorch paperback printing: October 2006

The stories contained in this volume appeared in *The Complete Western Stories of Elmore Leonard*, published in December 2004 by William Morrow, an imprint of HarperCollins Publishers.

HarperCollins®, HarperTorch™, and ♦™ are trademarks of Harper-Collins Publishers Inc.

Printed in the United States of America

Visit HarperTorch on the World Wide Web at www.harpercollins.com

10 9 8 7 6 5 4 3 2 1

☆ Contents ☆

ARIZONA TERRITORY 1880s

to WHIPPLE BARRACKS

Fort Apache

Fort McDowell

PHOENIX

Superstition Mountains

Apache Junction

Inspiration

Globe

San Carlos

San Carlos Apache Indian Reservation

Hatch & Hodges Central Mail Section

Gila River

Gila Ford

Rindo's Station

White Tanks

Gila Mountains

Pinaleno Mountains

Casa Grande

Florence

Fort Thomas

to YUMA

Fort Grant

to LAS CRUCES, NEW MEXICO

N
W E
S

San Pedro River

Fort Bowie

Dos Cabezas Mountains

Tucson

Willcox

Dos Cabezas

Benson

Dragoon Mountains

Canyon Diablo

Contention

Tombstone

Arivaca

Sasabe

Fort Huachuca

Sweetmary

Bisbee

Nogales

Douglas

Blood Money
and other stories

1

Apache Medicine

KLEECAN WAS THREE hours out of Cibicu, almost halfway to the Mescalero camp at Chevelon Creek, when he met the Apache.

Ordinarily he welcomed company, for the life of a cavalry scout is lonely enough without the added routine of riding from camp to camp to count reservation heads, and that day the sky was a dismal gray-green to the north, dark and depressing. It made the semidesert surroundings stand out in vivid contrast—the alkali stretches a garish white between low, bleak hills and ghostly, dust-covered mesquite clumps. It was a composite of gray and bright white and dead green that formed a coldness, a penetrating chill that was premature for so early in September, and more than anything else, it made a man feel utterly alone.

But even with the loneliness on him, Kleecan did not welcome the company he saw on the trail ahead. For he had recognized the Apache. It was Juan Pony. And Juan had been drinking mescal.

There wasn't a man in the vicinity of San Carlos who would have blamed Kleecan for not wanting to meet an Apache under such conditions—and especially this one. Juan Pony had a reputation for meanness, and he did everything in his power to keep the reputation alive. And because he was the son of Pondichay, chief of the Chevelon Creek Mescaleros, other Apaches kept out of his way and white men had to use special handling, for Pondichay had a reputation too.

Less than two years before, he had cut a path of fire and blood from Chihuahua to the Little Colorado, and it had taken seven troops of cavalry to subdue thirty-four braves. Twenty-eight civilians and thirteen troopers had been killed during the campaign. Pondichay had lost two men. He was not to be taken lightly; yet the Bureau had merely snatched his carbine from him and given him a few sterile acres of sand along the Chevelon.

Then the Bureau gave the carbine to Kleecan and turned its back, lest Kleecan had to use it to crush the hostile's skull. Pondichay was hungry for war, and he loved his son more than anything on the Apache earth. The least excuse would send Pondichay back on the warpath. That was why men kept out of the way of Juan Pony. But Kleecan had a job to do. He dropped his left elbow to feel the bulge of the handgun under his coat as he reined in before Juan Pony, who had turned his sorrel sideways, blocking the narrow trail.

★ ★ ★

THE SCOUT could have easily gone around, for the sandy ground was flat on both sides of the trail, but Kleecan had a certain standing to think of. When a man scouts for the cavalry and keeps track of reservation Apaches, he's boss, and he never lets the Apache forget it. Juan Pony had a poor memory, but he had to be reminded with a smile—for his father was still Pondichay.

The scout nodded his head. "*Salmann*, Juan."

Juan Pony shifted his position on the saddle blanket to show full face, but he ignored the scout's greeting of *friend*. Instead, he swung an old Burnside .54 carbine in the scout's direction, aimlessly but with the hint of a threat, and mumbled some words of Mescalero through tight lips. His sharp-featured face was drawn, and his eyes bloodshot, but through his drunkenness it was plain to see what was in his soul. An Apache does not sip mescal like a gentleman. Nor does it have the same effect.

Kleecan caught one of the mumbled words and it was not complimentary. He said, "Juan, you be a good boy and go home. You go on home and I won't report you for tippin' at the mescal."

The Apache nudged the sorrel with his right heel and the horse moved forward and to the side until the naked knee of the Apache was touching the top of the scout's calf-high boot. They were close, two feet separating their faces, and the scout could smell the foulness of the Apache. Rancid body odor and the sour smell of mescal—the result of a three-day binge.

Kleecan wanted to back away, but he sat motionless, his eyes fixed on the Apache's face, his own dark and impassive in the shadow of the narrow-brimmed hat. Kleecan had been smelling mescal and tizwin on the foul breaths of Apaches for almost fifteen years, and it occurred to him that it never did get any sweeter. He noticed a gleam of saliva at the corner of Juan Pony's mouth and he unconsciously passed a knuckle along the bottom of his heavy dragoon mustache.

He said, "I'll ride along with you, Juan. I'm goin' up to Chevelon to see your daddy." Juan Pony did not answer, but continued to stare at him, his eyes tightening into slits. He leaned closer to the scout until his face and coarse, loose-hanging hair were less than a foot from the scout's. Then Juan Pony cleared his throat and spat, full into the dark face beneath the narrow brim, and with it he sneered the word "*Coche!*" with all the hate in his savage soul.

In the desolate country north of San Carlos,

when a man meets a drunken Apache and the Apache spits in his face, he does one of two things: smiles, or shoots him.

KLEECAN SMILED. Because he was looking into the future. But with the smile there was a gnawing in his belly, a gnawing and a revulsion and a bitter urge rising within him that he could not stem by simply gritting his teeth. And though he was looking into the future and seeing Pondichay, fifteen years of dealing with the Apache his own way overruled five seconds of logic, and his hand formed a fist and he drove it into the sneering face of Juan Pony.

The Apache went backward off the sorrel, still clutching the carbine, and was out of sight the few seconds it took Kleecan's arm to rise and swing down against the rump of the sorrel. The horse bolted off to the side of the trail with the slap to reveal the Apache pushing himself up with one hand, raising the Burnside with the other. Instinct told Kleecan to draw the handgun, but the ugly, omnipotent face of Pondichay was there again and he flung himself from the saddle in one motion to land heavily on the rising form of Juan Pony. The Apache went backward, landing hard on his back, but his legs were doubled against his body and as he hit, one moccasin shot up between the scout's legs and kicked savagely.

Kleecan's fingers were at the Apache's throat, but the fingers stiffened and spread and he imagined a fire cutting through his body, pushing him away from the Indian. He was on his feet for a moment and then sickness rose from his stomach and almost gagged him so that he fell to his knees and doubled up, holding an arm close to his stomach. Juan Pony twisted his mouth into a smile in his drunkenness and raised the Burnside .54. It would tear a large hole in the white scout. He smiled and began to aim.

His cheek was against the smooth stock when he heard the explosion, and he looked up in surprise, for he was certain he had not yet fired. Then he saw the revolving pistol in the outstretched arm in front of him. Juan Pony had underestimated. It was the last thing he saw in his natural life.

It was said of Kleecan that he never let go. That after he was dead he would still take the time to get the man who had killed him, for Kleecan was not expected to die in bed. He dropped the pistol and rolled to his side with his knees almost touching his chest. The pain cut like a saber and with it was the feeling of sickness. But after a few minutes the saliva eased down from his throat and the sharp pain began to turn to a stiffness. He got to his feet slowly and took the first few steps as if he were walking over broken bottles without boots, but he looked at Juan Pony and the glance snatched him back to reality. And he looked with a grim, troubled face, for he knew what the death of the son of an Apache war chief could mean.

The sky was darker, still gray-green but darker, when Kleecan returned to his mare. He saw the storm approaching and the trouble-look seemed to lift slightly from his dark face. The rain would come and wash away the sign. But it would not wash away the urge for revenge in Pondichay, for the old chief was certain to find the body of his son, buried shallow beneath the rocks and brush off-trail. Pondichay would have no sign to explain to him how it had happened, but that would not hold his hand from its work of vengeance. A revenge on any and all that he chanced to meet. As soon as he discovered the bones of his son.

The scout had one leg up in a stirrup when he saw the small beaded deerskin bag in the road. A leather thong attached to it had been broken, and he realized he had ripped it from the Apache's throat when he had been kicked backward. He picked it up and looked the hundred-odd feet to the mesquite clump where he had buried Juan Pony. He hesitated only for a moment and then stuffed the bag into a side coat pocket. He rode off to the east, leading Juan Pony's sorrel. When he had gone almost three miles, he released the horse with a slap on the rump and set off at a gallop, still toward the east.

He pushed his mount hard, for he wanted to reach the Hatch & Hodges Station at Cottonwood

Creek before the rain came. Overhead, the sky was becoming blacker.

AT A QUARTER to four Kleecan stopped at the edge of the mesa. In front of him the ground dropped gradually a thousand yards or more to the adobe stagecoach station at Cottonwood Creek. He watched a Hatch & Hodges Concord start to roll, the greasers jump to the sides, and he could faintly hear the shouts of the driver as he reined with one hand and threw gravel at the lead horses with the other. Within a hundred feet the momentum was up and the Concord streaked past the low adobe wall that ringed the station house on four sides. The yells grew fainter and the dust trail stretched and puffed and soon the coach passed from view, following a bend in the Cottonwood, and all that was left was the cylinder of dust that rolled on to the north into the approaching blackness.

Somewhere in the stillness there was the cold-throated howl of a dog coyote. It complemented the dreary blackness pressing from the north like a soul in hell's despair. Kleecan stiffened in the saddle and started to the south into a yellowness that was sun-glare and hazy reflection from the northern storm, and with it the deathlike stillness. Then his eye caught motion. It was a speck, a blur against the yellow-gray, and he knew it to be the dust

raised from fast-moving horses. Probably four
miles off. Three, four horses. It was hard to tell in
the haze. When he reached the bottom of the grade
he could no longer see the dust, but he was sure the
riders had been heading for the Hatch & Hodges
Station.

Art McLeverty, the station agent, came out of the
doorway and stood under the front ramada,
scratching a massive stomach. His stubby fingers
clawed at a soiled expanse of blue-striped shirt, col-
larless, the neckband frayed, framing a lobster-red
neck and above it an even deeper red, puffy face.
Kleecan called it the map of Ireland because he had
heard the expression somewhere and knew McLeverty thought of it as a compliment.

McLeverty sucked in his stomach and yelled in
no particular direction, "Roberto! *¡Aquí muy
pronto!*" And almost at once a small Mexican boy
was in front of the mount, taking the reins from
Kleecan.

The station agent led the way through the doorway and then to the right to the small mahogany
bar that crossed one side of the narrow room. On
the opposite side of the doorway was the long plank
table and eight cane-bottomed Douglas chairs
where the stage passengers ate, and between bar
and table, against the back wall, was the rolltop
desk where McLeverty kept his accounts and
schedules. Bare, cold to the eye, grimy from sand

blowing through the open doorway, it was where Kleecan went for a drink when he had the time.

He leaned on the bar and took off his hat, rubbing the back of his hand over eyes and forehead. Thin, dark hair was smeared against the whiteness of a receding hairline, but an inch above the eyes the face turned tan and weather-beaten and the dragoon mustache, waxed at the tips, accentuated a face that could look ferocious as well as kindly. With his hat on, straight over his eyes, the brim cut a shadow of hardness over his face and Kleecan looked stern and cold. Without the hat he looked kindly because the creases at the corners of his eyes cut a perpetual smile in his light blue eyes. He dropped the hat back onto his head, loosely.

"Oh, guess I'll have mescal, Art." He said it slowly, as if after deliberation, though he drank mescal every time he came here.

The station agent reached for the bottle of pale liquid and set it in front of Kleecan, then picked up a thick tumbler and passed it against his shirt before placing it next to the bottle. McLeverty looked as if he was memorizing a speech. He was about to say something, but Kleecan had started to talk.

"If you'd slice up a hen and drop her into the mescal when it's brewin', you'd get a little tone to it. Damn white stuff looks like water." He was pouring as he spoke. He cleared his throat and drank down half a tumblerful.

"I don't make it, I only sell it." McLeverty said it hurriedly. He was almost puffing, so anxious to tell something he knew. "Listen, Kleecan! Didn't you hear the news—no, I know you didn't. . . ." And then he blurted it out: "The paymaster got robbed and killed this morning! Indians!" He had said it. Now he relaxed.

✯ ✯ ✯

KLEECAN HADN'T looked up. He poured another drink. "I'm not kiddin' with you, Art. You ought to watch the Mexes make it. Throw a few pieces of raw chicken in it and your mescal'll turn kind of a yellow. Makes it look like it's got some body."

"Damn it, Kleecan! I said the paymaster got robbed! The paywagon burned and the paymaster, Major Ulrich, and four of the guards shot and scalped as bald as you please. Passengers going up to Holbrook were all talking about it. They said a cavalry patrol'd stopped them on the road from Apache and told them and then asked them if they'd seen anything. And they were all scared to hell 'cause the cavalry lieutenant told them he was sure it was Juan Pony and some Mescaleros, 'cause no one's seen Juan in almost a week. Damn butchers are probably all up in the hills now."

Kleecan took another drink before looking at the Irishman. "What happened to the other two guards? They always ride at least six."

"They think they were carried away by the 'Paches. What else you think! They weren't around!"

"Art, there're only two things wrong with your story," he said. "Number one: Mescaleros don't scalp. You been out here long enough to know that. And it wouldn't be Yavapais, Maricopas, or Pimas, 'cause they've been farmin' so long their boys don't know what a scalp knife looks like—and an Arapaho hasn't been down this far in ten years. Number two: Just a little more than three hours ago I shot Juan Pony as dead as you can get. And he was too full of mescal to have taken any paymaster."

Kleecan pushed away from the bar and did a half kneebend. "Damn Indian like to ruined me for life."

McLeverty didn't know what to say. He stood behind the bar with his mouth slightly open and watched his story break up into little pieces.

The scout couldn't help smiling. When news reaches a man in a lonely corner like the Cottonwood station, he will tell it to himself over and over, savoring it, waiting, his jaw aching to tell it to the next man that comes in from an even farther corner. He was a little bit sorry he had spoiled the news-breaking for McLeverty.

Kleecan said, "Tell you what, Art. I'll bet you five to three dollars that there weren't any Indians around and that those two missin' guards are in on the deal."

As he spoke his gaze drifted along the front wall and then stopped at the wide window. There was the flat whiteness, the darkness above it, then in the distance the dust cloud. A few moments later he made out three horsemen. His eyes narrowed from habit, years of squinting into the distance, and he judged that two of the riders could be wearing cavalry blue.

"Get the Army up this way much, Art?"

McLeverty followed the scout's gaze out the window. He squinted for a long time, then his eyes became wider as the riders drew closer, and next they were bulging, for McLeverty seldom enough got a troop of cavalry on patrol up this way—let alone two troopers and a civilian—and it was easy to see he was thinking of what Kleecan had said about the other two guards being a part of the holdup.

And Kleecan was thinking of the same thing. He had been making conversation before. Now he wasn't sure. He told himself it was just the timing that made him think that way.

McLeverty couldn't turn his eyes from the window. He just stared. Finally he said, "God, do you suppose those three—"

"Four," Kleecan said. "I'll add another dollar that there're four of them."

★ ★ ★

TWO TROOPERS and a civilian, dressed for riding, came into the room slowly and glanced around before walking over to the bar. But even in their slight hesitancy they had smiled. They stood at the bar brushing trail dust from their coats, still smiling, and talked about the coming rain and the dark sky, and they offered to buy the station agent and the scout a drink. Kleecan didn't speak because he was trying to picture the happy world these men were living in. It wasn't cynicism. It was just that men didn't ride into an out-of-the-way stage station covered with the grime of hours on horseback and then suddenly react with a brotherly-love spirit that belonged to Christmas Eve. A saddle doesn't treat a man that way.

McLeverty was pushing the bottle across the bar to the three men when the back door opened and the fourth one entered. Like the other civilian his coat was open and a pistol hung at his side. McLeverty looked at the man and then to Kleecan and in the look there was a mixture of suspicion, respect, and fear.

The fourth man saw the suspicion.

"Wanted to use your backhouse," he explained. "Afore I came in and had to go right out again," and he ended the words with a meaningless laugh.

He joined the others at the bar and stood next to Kleecan, who lounged against the bar with his back half turned to the four men. The fourth one slapped the two troopers on the shoulders and told them to pour a drink. The troopers were younger than the two civilians. Big, rawboned men, they wore their uniforms slovenly and didn't seem to care. The man who had come in the back way did most of the talking and most of the drinking.

They had been at the bar for almost fifteen minutes when the lull finally came. They had been talking continually during that time. Talking about uninteresting things in loud voices. There were a few words, then prolonged laughter, and after that silence. The four men lifted their glasses to their lips. It was a way of filling the lull while they thought of something else.

Kleecan turned his head slightly in their direction. "Hear about the paymaster gettin' held up?"

When he said it four drinks were still mouth high. There was the clatter of a shot glass hitting the bar. And the strangled coughing as a drink caught halfway down a throat, and the continued coughing as the liquor hung there and burned. But after the coughing there was silence. Kleecan wasn't paying any attention to them.

The fourth man had his coat open and his right hand was on the pistol butt at his hip. The two troopers glanced at each other and then at Kleecan, who had turned his head in their direction, but they dropped the glance to somewhere in front of them. Only the other civilian was completely composed. He hadn't moved a muscle. He was about Kleecan's age, older than the other three, and wore long dragoon mustaches similar to the scout's.

He looked at Kleecan. "No, mister. Tell us about it. Happen near here?" The man's voice was even, and carried a note of curiosity.

"Happened south of Fort Apache," Kleecan said. "That right, Art?"

McLeverty said, "That's right. The major was coming up from Fort Thomas when these—uh—Indians jumped the train and took five scalps and the pay."

"You don't say," the civilian said. "We've just come from Fort McDowell. Left yesterday and been riding ever since. That's why we haven't heard anything, I guess." He smiled, but not with nervousness.

Kleecan didn't smile. He nodded to the troopers. "You soldiers from Whipple?"

"Yes, they're both from Whipple Barracks." The civilian answered before either trooper could say anything. "You see, my partner and I are to join the survey party on the upper Chevelon, and these two gentlemen"—he pointed to the two troopers with a sweep of his arm—"are our guides."

"You could use another guide," Kleecan said. "You're fifteen miles east of Chevelon."

The civilian looked dumbfounded. He pushed his hat back from his forehead. "No! Why I thought it was due north of here!" There was surprise in his voice. "Well, it's a good thing we stopped in here," he said. "You say we have to go back fifteen miles?"

Kleecan didn't answer. He was staring at the troopers, looking at the regiment number on their collars. And as he looked he couldn't help the feeling that was coming over him. "I didn't know the Fifth was over at McDowell," he said.

The civilian shrugged his shoulders. "You know how the Army moves regiments around."

"I ought to," Kleecan said slowly. "I guide for them."

The silence was heavy in the narrow room. Heavy and oppressing, and because no one spoke the silence acted to strip naked the thoughts of the two men who stood at the bar staring into each other's eyes. The civilian knew his pretense was at an end and he shrugged his shoulders again, but looked in Kleecan's face.

Kleecan stared back at him, and all of a sudden there was a god-awful hate in him and he wanted to yell something, swear, and go for his gun—because the Fifth was at Fort Thomas, and the paywagon guards would be men of the Fifth, but they wouldn't wear their forage caps like that, not without the slant across an eye that meant Manassas and Antietam and a thousand miles of blood-red plains between the Rosebud and the Gila, and there was no survey party on the upper Chevelon for he had taken it out ten days before, and two men didn't go into Mescalero country to survey with two others who pretended to be troopers—not without equipment.

The civilian said, matter-of-factly, "What are you going to do about it?"

Kleecan stood motionless and knew he couldn't do anything about it. But he felt the hot anger drain from his face and he was glad of that, for then he wouldn't move rashly. Four to one wasn't gambling odds.

"Well, if you don't know, I'll tell you," the civilian said. "You're going to get on your horse and start guiding, and you're going to guide us over the best trail right out of Arizona, and you'll ride with that feeling that the least little move you make out of line will be your last. If we go, you go, and you don't look like a martyr to me."

* * *

THE RAIN CONTINUED to drizzle in the early dusk. They rode single file along the narrow trail that followed the bend of the lower Chevelon, and they rode in silence, each man with his own thoughts. Kleecan was soaked to the skin. One of the troopers had taken his poncho and now rode huddled, his chin bent into the folds of the collar, his body dry. When it had started to grow dark, Kleecan thought they would stop and find some kind of shelter for the night. He had even suggested it, but

the outlaw leader had only laughed and said,
"Travel when it's raining and there isn't any sign.
You ought to know that, Indian scout. We'll keep
on long as the rain lasts, even if we ride all night."
That had been almost two hours before.

And it was then that the idea had been born.
Even if we ride all night. He had had two hours to
think it out clearly.

When they came to the Chevelon ford it was almost dark. Kleecan dismounted and walked to the
bank of the running creek that was now almost
waist deep from the continuous rain. The outlaw
leader dismounted with him, but the others stayed
on their horses, back under the bow of a cottonwood. From there the two men at the creek bank
were only dim shadows. And that was what
Kleecan was counting on. He looked at the creek
and then to the outlaw and nodded his head, but as
he turned to go back to his horse his foot slipped
on the loose, sandy bank, throwing him off balance
and hard against the outlaw. The man pushed
Kleecan aside violently and drew his gun in a clean
motion, but not before Kleecan's hand had found
the side pocket of his coat.

"Don't do that again. We don't need you that bad."

"The darkness is makin' you spooky. I slipped on
the bank."

Nothing more was said.

They made the crossing without mishap and

picked up the trail again on the other side. In the darkness they made their way haltingly, brushing sharp chaparral and ducking suddenly as the blackness of a tree limb loomed in front of their faces. Kleecan rode silently and gave no warning call when an obstruction came in the trail, then smiled when he'd hear the curse from one of the outlaws whose face had been swatted by a soaked tree branch. The rain continued to drizzle and they rode on. They were a good two miles from the creek ford when Kleecan called back, "Trail goes left." Then he kicked the mare hard and swerved her to the left to follow the sharp turn in the trail.

The outlaws were taken by surprise momentarily. Their heads were down, shielding their faces from the stinging drizzle, but they heard Kleecan's mare break into a gallop, and in a body they spurred their own horses, bunching in confusion at the trail bend, then singling out to kick their mounts into a gallop up a sharp, widening rise. The trail dipped again suddenly and the outlaw chief, in the lead, reined in with a jolting motion, swinging an arm over his head. In the dimness he saw heavy, bulky shapes all around him, round and massive. The outlaws instinctively brought their mounts in close together and looked about, squinting into the darkness. Then one of the outlaws made a noise like a deep sigh. It was a moan and an exclamation. Somebody said, "Oh, God!" and another man cursed, but it sounded like a prayer, for there was a plea in it. On the outer rim they saw the hazy shapes of the wickiups and on four sides of them they looked down into the faces of Mescalero Apaches.

Kleecan had led them into the middle of Pondichay's rancheria.

The scout still sat his mare, but he was beyond the circle of Apaches. Next to him stood Pondichay, old and somber, too polite to ask outright the meaning of the sudden intrusion. Kleecan greeted him in Mescalero and continued to speak in that tongue, but he kept his eyes on the outlaw chief as he spoke.

For Kleecan told the old chief many things. He told him what a great warrior he was and recounted many of Pondichay's deeds, but slowly his voice saddened and finally he told him how sad he had been to hear of Juan Pony. The old Apache looked up, but Kleecan continued. And he told him that Juan Pony had been murdered. He told him that he had worked great medicine and was able to bring right to this camp the murderers of Juan Pony. His voice became cold and he told him how the murderers had committed the greatest sacrilege of all by taking Juan's *hoddentin* sack, which held the sacred pollen to ward off evil. And he told Pondichay that if he did not believe him, why not look in the chief murderer's pocket and see if the

medicine bag was not still there—for it is said that
an Apache warrior parts with his *hoddentin* bag
only when he is dead.

Kleecan wheeled his horse around. He had made
his offering to the gods of destruction.

Red Hell Hits Canyon Diablo

THEY CALLED IT Canyon Diablo, but for no apparent reason. Like everything else it had advantages and disadvantages, good points and bad ones, depending on the time of the day, the season of the year, or who happened to be occupying the canyon at a given time. At this particular time, two hundred feet up the south wall, a solitary disadvantage stood motionless on the narrow ledge, watching the small group of riders on the open plain approach the dark defile that led into the canyon. A dozen feet above his head the rock sloped back abruptly straightening into the flat tableland. Directly below, the wall extended in a sheer drop to the canyon mouth; but a few yards to his right the canyon wall buckled with loose rock and thorn brush, sloping gradually out into the open plain.

A fifty caliber buffalo rifle rested on a waist-high boulder in front of him, pointed in the general direction of the riders. His gaze followed the same line, his face motionless, though the sand-specked hot wind nudged shoulder-length, jet-black hair and forced his eyelids to lower slightly, so that he watched with eyes that were slits against the glare. Eyes that were small, black, bullet-like . . . staring at the riders with a cold-steel hate. It is easy for a Chiricahua Apache to hate. It is doubly so when his vision is filled with the sight of *blanco* horse soldiers.

Lieutenant Gordon Towner reined in his patrol at the signal from the rider fifty yards ahead. Matt Cline, the civilian scout, wheeled his pony and rode back to the officer and six men.

"Did you see him, Lieutenant?"

"Did I see whom?"

Matt Cline's jaw bulged, a wad of tobacco accentuating his creased, ruddy face, and the short brim of his hat was low on his forehead casting a shadow to the tips of his straggly, black mustache. His lips were parted slightly by the tobacco bulge of his jaw and barely moved when he spoke. He pointed ahead to the mouth of the canyon three hundred yards away, and then his arm swept up to the top of the south wall. Pointing up, his lean, heavily veined arm stretched from the sleeve of red flannel underwear. He wore no shirt. His suspenders crossed the sweat-stained, colorless undershirt and attached to dark serge trousers that tucked into high, dust-caked boots. Across his lap he held a Remington-Hepburn.

"See that ledge runnin' along near the top of the wall? Well, not a minute ago one of our little friends was up there." The scout ended with a stream of tobacco juice spurting into the white dust.

The lieutenant pulled the brim of his floppy, gray field hat closer to his eyes and squinted ahead to the canyon entrance. A hundred things raced through his mind, and every one of them was a question. It was his patrol and he was supposed to have the answers. That's why he had a commission. But the face bore a puzzled expression. It was young, and lobster-red, and told openly that he was new to frontier station, though he had learned all the answers at the Point. You hesitate when it's your command, your responsibility. When a dirty old man in an undershirt is studying you to see what you've got, waiting to pick you apart. And if he finds the wrong thing, the buzzards do the rest of the picking.

"Mr. Cline, the primary objective of this patrol is to locate and bring in Trooper Byerlein. If in the process we come across hostiles, it is also the duty of this patrol to scout them and deal with them using the best means at hand. I would judge that there is a ranchería somewhere in that canyon. I don't think their band could be very large, for I know of no Indians at San Carlos that are unaccounted for.

Now that we've found one, or possibly a band, we'll have to act quickly before they get away."

"You got it wrong there, Lieutenant," the scout said. "We didn't find him. That Indian found us."

"Perhaps I'm wrong, but I'd observe him to be a lookout. Now he's obviously fled after being seen."

"Only thing wrong with that, Lieutenant, is that you don't observe an Apache when he's on lookout. I don't know what your experience is, but I hear this is your first patrol out of Fort Thomas. You might as well learn right now that when you spot an Apache like that, it's because he wants you to see him. Right now there could be a dozen of 'em hidin' on that rocky grade goin' up to the ledge. If we was to ride to the mouth we'd see him again just a little way further on. Then you'd go further and you'd see him again. Until he led you to the right spot. There'd be a lot of shots and you'd go back to Thomas draped over your horse facedown. If there's anybody left to lead the horse."

And so they learned. The lieutenant faced the scout, but was silent. It wasn't the best thing to have been said in front of his men. Above all, they had to have confidence in him. He waited until he felt the heat of embarrassment drain from his face.

"What do you suggest, then?"

Matt Cline shifted his chew to the other cheek. "Well, it looks like Byerlein's tracks go into the canyon, which means they pro'bly got him. It's one thing trackin' a deserter, but it's another goin' into an Apache rancheria to get him. If he's there he's either dead or half dead, so there's no worry there anymore." He pointed to a splash of green that crept between low hills to the north of where they were standing.

"I think we'd better wait and move over to those pines until Sinsonte shows up. He'll cut our sign over to there without any trouble. Maybe he'll know just what we're up against."

★ ★ ★

FROM THE EDGE of the pines they watched the canyon entrance across the empty stretch of desert, and the shadowy defile that slashed into the mountainside had eight different meanings. But it flicked through everyone's mind that it was a place where you could die while never seeing what did it. Six enlisted troopers prayed to six interpretations of God that the young lieutenant wasn't a glory seeker . . . at least not on this patrol. So the men sprawled in sand and grass, their bodies relaxed—though it's a singular type of relaxation only a little more than a mile from the Apache. Eyes are ever watchful. The lieutenant and Cline sat a little apart from the men. Towner pulled at the sparse tufts of grass nervously, looking around in every direction, but mostly toward the canyon.

"How do you know you can trust Sinsonte?" It

was more than just making conversation. "He's an Apache just like the rest of them. How do you know he isn't eating with that band of hostiles right now?"

"Well, for one thing, army chow's spoiled him," the scout answered. "He probably wouldn't even touch mescal anymore if somebody baked it for him. I been scoutin' with him goin' on five years now and I don't have any reason not to trust him. The day he turn around and lets go with his Sharps at me, why, then I'll quit trustin' him."

Cline smiled at his joke. "'Course he ain't always been a scout. He was with Cochise ten years ago, shootin' all the whites he could, long as he needed a pony or a few extra rounds, but that was just somethin' in his past. To an Apache, what you did a long time ago hasn't got much bearin' on what you happen to be doin' at the present. And I don't think he got along too well with Cochise, though he was with him since Apache Pass. 'Course, he won't come right out and tell you. See, Sinsonte is a White Mountain Apache, and for some reason—buried somewhere in his past—he's got a full-fledged hate for Chiricahuas. That, along with army rations, is why he's the best tracker at Fort Thomas."

"Uh-huh," Towner grunted. "So you think the hostiles in the canyon are Chiricahuas." It was half question, half statement of fact. The words of a brand-new lieutenant, willing to learn, but wishing he could have picked his own instructor.

Cline said, "I don't see how they could be anythin' else. If they're all accounted for on the reservation, then they must be ones that come up from across the border. When we was roundin' up the bands to bring them to San Carlos and Fort Apache, a bunch of 'em slipped through the net and streaked south for the Sierra Madres, and nobody could dig 'em out of those hills. Now, every once in a while, bands of 'em come raidin' back into Arizona for horses and shells. They're carryin' on a little war with the Mexicans and have to keep their supplies up. Everybody'd just as soon they never come back. They got some good leaders . . . Chatto, Nachez, old Nana and Loco. And now I hear about an upstart medicine man who's gainin' influence. Name's Geronimo. I'd bet the bucks over in that canyon are part of that band."

An hour after sundown, Lieutenant Towner was still sitting at the edge of the pines, repeatedly shifting from one position to another on the sandy ground. Pine-tree shadows striped his soft face and made his eyes seem to shine. They were open wide. It was a long way from Springfield, Mass. A few yards out in the desert there was a muffled scraping sound, and he jumped to his feet, tugging at his holstered revolving pistol. By the time he had gotten it out, Sinsonte was standing next to him. Matt Cline came up from somewhere behind him.

"Did you find 'em?"

Sinsonte stood in front of his pony holding the hackamore close under the animal's head, while the other hand still covered the nostrils. A man can be shot even when approaching a friendly camp.

"I find, nantan." Sinsonte, a little man even for an Apache, stood with narrow, hunched shoulders. He was perhaps fifty years and his eyes were beginning to be rivered with tiny red lines, but in them still was a fire, a fire that belonged to a younger man. Besides the calico red band holding his hair in place, he wore only high Apache moccasins with turned-up toes and a white cotton breechclout. A uniform jacket was lashed in his bedroll for more peaceful days.

The two scouts crouched together at the edge of the desert for a long time, drawing obscure lines in the sand and conversing in a mixture of Apache and Spanish with only an occasional English word. For a few minutes the lieutenant leaned over their map of sand, trying to recognize a mark or hear even a part of their conversation that was understandable. Finally he turned away in disgust.

"Sergeant Lonnigan!" The old sergeant rose from the circle of enlisted men. "Issue half rations all around. No fire. Therefore no coffee." It felt good to bark an order.

Dammit, he was still in command!

"Yes, sir!" Lonnigan snapped his reply. Thirty years in the army. Seven years longer than the shavetail had even existed. But Lonnigan was used to young second lieutenants. He had served under many. He remembered one who was now a general. He remembered two during the march to the sea, and at Shiloh—they were both colonels. And he remembered dozens of others who were dead. For some reason he liked this new Lieutenant Towner, even if he was too straight out of the manual and didn't know much about Apaches. He remembered a time not too long ago when he himself had never heard the name Apache. You learned. And there are little humps of ground out behind the commissary building at Thomas to testify for those who didn't.

In a little while Cline went over to the lieutenant.

"Sinsonte found them. Chiricahuas. He was only a few dozen yards from that lookout who tried to lure us in, and he followed him. When the lookout saw the lure wouldn't work, he headed straight for the camp to talk it over with the rest of 'em. About fourteen, fifteen. Sinsonte says from Nachez's band, but they're here with a subchief by the name of Lacayuelo . . . and mister, he's really a bad one. He's even hard in the eyes of most of the Apaches, and that's sayin' somethin'. I'd guess the rest of 'em are bad actors just like he is."

"Did he see Byerlein?"

"Yeah, but he was layin' on the ground in the

middle of 'em, so Sinsonte don't know if'n he's alive or dead. I'd say he's half of either one."

The lieutenant looked out through the dingy grayness of the moonbathed desert to the black slash that was Canyon Diablo, reflecting on what he had been told. It made it no easier for him, but he turned to the scout abruptly.

"Mr. Cline, if Sinsonte can sneak up on a band of hostiles without being detected, then he can lead this patrol in. Perhaps not to their camp, but at least to a favorable position from which we can make contact without being at a disadvantage. An ever present obligation to prevent the hostiles from committing further depredations in the Territory cannot be turned aside or put off. My duty is before me, Mr. Cline, and will be carried out whether you object or not." He paused to give emphasis to his words. "So we're going to get them."

"I don't object, mister. You're the boss. I knew ever since this afternoon that you'd be wantin' to go in, so Sinsonte and I just did a little figurin' and I think we got an answer."

"How to get in?"

"Yeah," the scout replied. "Sinsonte's leavin' now to snake acrost that open stretch. In about four hours the moon'll be down low enough for the rest of us to get acrost. We leave the horses here. And I say take all the men along, no horse guard left behind, 'cause we'll need all the carbines we got. 'Course that's up to you. The idee is to angle from here so as to land us on the north side of the mountain, three miles up from the entrance we saw this afternoon. On the north it slopes up pretty gradual, and there's a trail that winds about half-way up and then cuts down into rocky country and on into the center of the canyon. The trail in's a fair hard one to find, but Sinsonte's goin' to meet us where it starts. He's out layin' the carpet now."

Chapter Two

The White Flag

The moon claimed it was near three o'clock when Cline halted the seven cavalrymen on a broad ledge halfway up the mountain slope. It had been hours since anyone had spoken. Neither the tedious climb nor the circumstance allowed for talk. Only once a teeth-clenched curse followed a misstep, and Towner turned long enough to glare at the trooper and curse him out with his eyes. Now could be heard the heavy breathing as each man stretched his neck to gulp the cool mountain air. Below them the desert rolled dimly for miles, and in the distance was a darker shadow. The clump of pines they had left hours before. From the ledge where they stood, a narrow defile slashed into the mountainside, its rock-wall sides rising over a hundred feet. The trail twisted from view thirty-odd yards ahead.

Cline said, "You never see the end of this one until you're there. She bends around so much."

Towner studied the approach. "You followed it before?"

"A few years back, but I don't look forward to walkin' down that aisle not knowin' who I'm goin' to meet." He looked around restlessly. "It beats me where Sinsonte is. If he don't show in ten minutes, we'll have to go on. This ain't no place to be perched when the sun comes out."

By five, the small band had threaded deep into the defile. Sinsonte had not come. The narrow passage had widened considerably, but it was a slow, exerting grind over the sharp rock and through the biting chaparral clumps that dotted the way. Towner had ordered absolute silence, but the order could not mute the metallic scrape of issue boots on hard rock or the rattle of stones kicked along the pathway. They kept their lips sealed and bit off the urge to curse out the army, the Apache, the sun-bleached country and Lieutenant Towner.

They were experienced men, combining one hundred and sixteen years of active service, and they knew what it was to walk up to an enemy. Walking slowly. How to march without speaking, without thinking, the vigilance being inbred. Many soldiers experienced it, but you had to fight Apaches to really know what it meant. Walking down a narrow trail in the heart of a Chiricahua stronghold, a soldier will even smile at the thought of the arid, glaring, baked-sand parade at Fort Thomas. There is a feeling of security there, though you wouldn't go so far as to call it home.

And Gordon Towner had his thoughts. Did Cook say anything about a similar circumstance? It was true, he was afraid, but more of doing the wrong thing, giving the wrong command, than of the Indians. A twenty-three-year-old boy from Springfield, leading his first command against an enemy, Chiricahua Apaches. A command that consisted of a sergeant, five privates and a grizzly old scout who would have to learn more respect for an officer of the United States Army.

The single file column stopped abruptly at the sign of Matt Cline's arm raised above his head. The trail narrowed again to less than ten feet across, and the path was partially blocked by clumps of thick bushes; but it was evident that they were near the end of the passage. Cline was moving ahead to scout the brush when the low moan of a single Apache voice reached them. The scout stopped dead and the voice went on in a broken-tongue chant, groans mixed with the chopped Apache words. He listened for a minute and recognized the death chant and went on, knowing what to expect.

Towner watched him approach the thick bushes and then stop and look to the right. He took a step toward the wall where a pile of loose boulders jutted out into the path, but stopped long enough to wave the others ahead. Behind the jutting rocks, in a shallow niche in the wall, Sinsonte sat propped against the wall mumbling the death chant through lips smeared with blood. At first glance, it looked as if his whole face had been lacerated, but in another second Towner saw that all the blood poured from his eyes, or where his eyes had been. He moved his legs stretched out in front of him and the feet wobbled loosely, turning too far to the sides, uncontrolled, the way they will when the tendons have been slashed. Sinsonte would never follow another sign.

Cline lifted his revolving pistol and placed it in the old Indian's hand, but he turned quickly to Towner who was looking the other way, swallowing hard to keep down the bile that was rising in his stomach.

"Come on, we got to get out of here." He was about to say more but his sentence was cut short by the singing ricochet of a bullet over their heads.

"They're behind us!" Lonnigan shouted and turned bringing his carbine up.

"Hold your fire, Sergeant! Everybody up!" Towner

had his handgun out and waved the men ahead with it. He waited until they had all followed Cline through the bushes, and then sprinted after them.

They scrambled over the rocks into the boulder-strewn clearing, glancing uncertainly at the four canyon walls that seemed to stretch to the sky, offering no avenue of escape. From somewhere to the left a volley of shots split the stillness scattering the soldiers behind the handiest bits of cover. Low clumps of mesquite dotted the clearing, but offered no permanent protection to the troopers.

Matt Cline took a snap shot at a mound of rock and brush fifty yards away over which a thin wisp of smoke was rising, then shouted to the lieutenant to spread the men out and follow him. It took him only a few seconds to grasp the situation and decide what course to take. There was only one choice. With the men behind him, Cline raced for a small clump of trees that grew out from between the rocks at the base of the right side of the box canyon, directly across from where the shots were coming.

Their backs were to the Indians firing from the well-concealed places along the left wall, but they ran well spread out, dodging and ducking, continually changing course to offer as difficult a target as possible. The firing was intense during the fifteen or twenty seconds it took them to reach the trees, but then died off abruptly as the last man vaulted the natural rock barrier and dropped among the trees. Not a hit. It was always a consoling thought that the Apaches never had bullets enough to waste on practice.

★　★　★

THEY TOOK CROUCHED positions five to ten feet apart behind the natural barricade of rocks and trees, pointing their carbines out between the rocks. And they waited. At their backs, the jagged canyon wall, veined with crevices and ledges, loomed skyward.

The lieutenant searched the cliff with his gaze, but could see the top in only one place through the dense trees. Apaches could get up there, but they wouldn't see anyone to fire on. No, the danger was ahead, among the rocks not three hundred yards away—and you couldn't see it. But he was satisfied with his position. It was small, right under the wall and not more than thirty yards wide. It wasn't a position you could hold forever, not without food and water. Still, the young officer was satisfied. There was no place the scout could lead them.

He nudged Cline. "Do you think they'll try to run over us?" He spoke in a low voice, as if afraid the Indians would overhear.

Cline shifted his chew, looking out over the clearing. He only occasionally glanced at the lieutenant. "Mister, I've known Apaches all my life—I even lived with them when I was a boy—but don't ask me what I think they'll do. Nobody knows what an Apache's goin' to do until it's done. I don't think even the Apache himself knows. But," the scout reflected, "I know they ain't goin' to come whoopin' across that open space if it means some of 'em gettin' killed. He's a heller, but he don't stick his neck out."

"Lieutenant!"

Towner and the scout crouched low and crawled to the trooper who had called.

"I think they're comin'. I seen somethin' move," the trooper said, pointing. "About twenty feet from the other side."

The scout squinted hard through the low branches. "Hell, yeah, they're comin'! Look!"

An Apache showed himself for a split second, disappearing into a shallow gully near the spot where the trooper had pointed. Cline threw up the Remington-Hepburn at the same time and fired, the bullet kicking up sand where the Indian had disappeared. "You got to shoot fast or there's nothin' to shoot at." The last word was on his lips when he threw the piece up again and fired.

"Damn, they move fast!"

Individually, then, the soldiers began firing at the darting, crawling, shadowy figures that never remained in sight more than a few seconds. They fired slowly, taking their time, with a patience that started for some of them at the first Bull Run. They knew what they were doing. They knew how to make each shot mean something.

From the opposite ridge came a heavy fire, continuing for almost a minute, keeping the soldiers crouching low behind their defenses.

"Keep shooting, dammit!" Towner screamed down the line. "They're moving up under fire cover!"

He turned to his own position in time to see the blur of a painted face and a red calico band loom in front of him not twenty feet away. The Apache was screaming, coming straight on, bringing a Sharps to his shoulder when Towner raised his handgun and fired. The face disappeared in a crimson flash, and for a split second a picture of Sinsonte passed through his mind. He stared between the rocks where the painted face had been. He saw it still. Gordon Towner had killed his first man . . . and sometimes it will do something to you.

Cline called over, "Good shootin', mister." But Towner didn't hear. He was squeezing off on another creeping shadow. He had been baptized.

They were firing continuously now, seeing more Apaches than there actually were. Every few minutes someone would yell, "I got one!" but most of their bullets whined harmlessly off the rocks and into the brush and sand. On to the middle of the day the cavalrymen pecked away in this fashion, firing sporadically at every cover that might conceal an Indian.

They were holding their own, successfully keeping the hostiles at bay, whittling down their number, except for one disastrous occurrence. An Apache who had crawled unbelievably close, was shot through the side as he dove for a cover, but the bullet did not stop him. He leaped to his feet and goaded himself on with a frenzied scream that brought him to the top of the barricade. If he was going to die, he didn't intend to die alone.

It all happened in a few seconds. Private Huber jumped up just as the Indian fired his heavy buffalo gun from the waist, and the ball caught the trooper square in the throat. At least four shots ripped through the Indian's body as he swung the heavy rifle like a club and smashed it against the side of a head. He teetered for a moment and then fell forward, still clutching the Sharps, onto the lifeless bodies of Privates Huber and Martz.

And when a man says one cavalryman is worth ten Apaches, he is a fool. It is certain he was not at Canyon Diablo that July day in '78.

SHORTLY AFTER NOON the firing slackened gradually and finally died out altogether. Not an Apache was in sight. They were certain that at least two or

three were still out in the middle somewhere, but if
they were, the devil himself was hiding them. A hot
breeze sang through the canyon, shifting the sand
and stirring the mesquite clumps. The movement of
the wind was all the more eerie contrasted with the
dead stillness of the canyon. There was not a human sound. The sun struck fiercely into the boxed
area, the shimmering heat waves mixing with the
sand-specked breeze to form a gritty element that
you could almost stick with a bayonet. It was hot,
blistering hot, and the lack of water made it all the
worse. That, and the overpressing reality that out
there, somewhere, were Apaches, Chiricahua
Apaches with the smell of blood in their nostrils. It
set a stage of silence and tortuous, eye-strained
waiting.

Towner and Cline squatted next to the two heaps
of stones that covered the dead cavalrymen. Since
burying Huber and Martz they had spoken less and
less. It was getting late in the afternoon. The silence
and back-breaking vigilance clung all the heavier,
daring conversation or a moment of relaxation. But
Towner was getting tired.

"If we ever get out of here I'll send back for them
to be buried at Thomas," he said.

"I don't think they'd care one way the other
now," the scout replied. "I know I wouldn't. What
difference does it make if . . . Well, I'll be damned!
Look at that!"

Matt Cline jumped up and pointed with his carbine toward the other side of the canyon. A white flag waved a few times above the grayness of rock, then an Indian stepped cautiously into the open carrying the flag tied to the end of an antiquated Springfield.

As he advanced, five Apaches jumped down from low ledges along the wall, and as they walked slowly toward Towner's position, three more Apaches appeared as if out of nowhere to join them. They had been hiding in the open area since giving up the sneak attack hours before. As the soldiers watched them advance, they wondered how the devil they could have missed seeing the three hiding right out in the open. Towner wondered if it wasn't just an excuse to gather up the warriors who had been stranded. Matt Cline wondered if the Springfield that bore the white flag was loaded.

The nine Apaches were still a few dozen yards away. Matt Cline leaned toward the lieutenant.

"I figure they're out of bullets or they wouldn't be playin' games. I'd say they want to get close, catch us off guard and finish the job with knives. If they had shells they could sit back there for a week and wait for us to come out in the open or die of starvation. It's gotta be a trick. Whatever you do, for God's sake don't trust 'em!"

Towner held his revolving pistol at his side. "Which one's Lacayuelo?"

"That little one with the cavalry jacket on, next to the one carryin' the flag."

A few feet from the defense line the Apaches stopped and Lacayuelo came on alone. His brown chest and stomach showed through the opening of the filthy, buttonless jacket. An empty cartridge belt crossed his chest and left shoulder. And an inane grin showed protruding teeth, forming a parallel with a smear of yellow paint that extended from ear to ear across the bridge of his nose. Like the others of his band he wore Apache moccasins that reached to his knees; but unlike the others whose only covering were light breechclouts, he wore ragged, gray trousers that tucked into his moccasins. His headband, holding back shoulder-length black hair, had once been a bright red, but now was a grease-stained, colorless rag. Three of the others wore small bush clumps attached to their headbands. At two hundred yards you wouldn't see them.

Lacayuelo began gesturing and speaking rapidly in the choppy, sound-picture Apache tongue. Matt Cline listened without interrupting, until he was finished, and then turned to the lieutenant.

"To make it short, he says there's no reason why we can't all be friends. He says just give him and his warriors some shells so they can hunt and keep from going hungry, and everybody'll be happy. He says he can't understand why we attacked him and his peaceful huntin' party."

Towner stared at the Apache. He took his campaign hat off and shook his head. "Does this animal understand English?"

"Enough to get by, but it would take him till Christmas to tell you anything."

The lieutenant continued to stare at Lacayuelo and his eyes narrowed. "Tell him he can go to hell with his hunting. He and his party are under arrest. Tell him he's going back to San Carlos to stand trial for murder."

Cline passed it on to the Chiricahua subchief who grinned and replied in only a few words.

"He says you can't arrest him, because he's here under the protection of a white flag. He says you have too much honor to disregard his sign of truce. He's a sly old devil, throwin' it back in your lap."

"Ask him what he's done with Byerlein."

The scout turned from the Indian after a minute. "He says he doesn't know what you're talkin' about. He says we're the first *blancos* he's seen in two months."

"He does, does he." Towner had not taken his eyes from the subchief since he stepped forward. Now, still looking full into his face, he raised his revolving pistol and pulled back the hammer. "Tell Lacayuelo that white flag or no white flag, I'll shoot his damn eyes out if he doesn't start talking about Byerlein."

Cline hesitated. "Mister, he's got more men than we have."

"He's got more men without bullets. Tell him!"

Cline passed it on and the words made the Apache lurch forward a half a step, but he looked into the muzzle of Towner's gun and stopped dead. He studied the young lieutenant, looking him up and down, taking his own good time; and finally must have decided that the *blanco* wasn't joking, for all at once a broad grin creased his evil, sun-scarred face and he was as friendly as could be. He jabbered to Cline for almost two minutes and then turned abruptly and walked away. The other Apaches followed.

"Where the devil are they going?"

Cline said, "He says he sees you're a friend of the Apache, so he's invitin' us to his rancheria for some refreshments. We're supposed to follow. He's thinkin' of somethin'. I say stay here."

Towner only glanced at him. "When you're in command, Mr. Cline, you can say that. Lonnigan! Spread out behind me. Mr. Cline, you'll walk at my side."

Five cavalrymen and a civilian scout walked slowly across the canyon floor, following the Indians by fifty yards. The sun had begun to drop behind the western canyon wall so that half of the boxed area was in shadow. Towner and the rest strode from the dark into the light and followed the Indians to the other side, then through a narrow defile into a side canyon. They walked into this new clearing where four wickiups stood and a dozen or so ponies were tethered on the other side of the canyon meadow. And they approached the Apaches with almost a swagger, a show of indifference, for they were cavalrymen of the "5th" . . . though they had only nine bullets between them.

Chapter Three

Tizwin

For an Apache rancheria, this one was comparatively clean, but it only testified that the Indians had not been there very long. The four wickiups were in a semicircle, and two cook fires, close together, were in the center of the half-moon area. Lacayuelo and his warriors sat in an irregular circle between the wickiups and the dead cook fires. He rose to one knee as they approached and beckoned them to join the circle; but Towner stopped the group on the opposite side of the cook fires and watched the Indians pass from one to the next a bulging water bag made from horse intestines.

Towner turned his head slightly. "What are they drinking?"

"Tizwin, most likely," Cline said. "Or mescal."

He watched the Indians drink. "I wouldn't put any pesos on it bein' water."

"What the devil's tizwin?"

"Apache corn beer. Knock you back to the States if you drink enough. Makes a worse Indian out of a bad one. I don't know what it'll do to a hardcase like Lacayuelo. He wants us to join 'em."

"Corn beer, eh," the lieutenant muttered, almost to himself. And he had a most uncommon look in his eyes.

Sometimes it seems as if certain men are set aside to do great things while others have to play the role of the fool or the coward, predestined from all eternity. But if you look close into every case, and that means everybody in the world, you'll see a time, a circumstance where a judgment has to be made that either makes or breaks the man. Sometimes luck helps. But it happens often in the army—especially on frontier station—and it was happening now to young Gordon Towner. Fortunately, he knew it. And wasn't afraid to push his luck.

"Mr. Cline, tell the filthy scoundrel that we'll be only too happy to join his soiree." And then to Lonnigan, "Sergeant, turn your bully boys loose. They can drink all they want—long as it's more than the Indians."

They sat where they had stood, on the other side of the ashes of the cook fires, ten to fifteen feet from the Apaches. Lacayuelo sent the water bag over to them—it turned out to be tizwin—but gestured and argued loudly for almost an hour for the *blancos* to join his circle. He was drinking all the time, like everyone else, and finally gave up his pleading when he saw that it was no use. The fly would not venture into the web. Perhaps he felt that ten feet wasn't far anyway.

The soldiers raised their baked-clay cups drink for drink with the Indians, carbines or handguns across laps, eyes ever watchful over the cup brims. It was a strange setting: the savage and the soldier, mortal enemies, drinking tizwin together, each watching for the false move. But the strangest sight was Gordon Towner. He was at least two cupfuls ahead of everyone else. He repeatedly drank down the warm liquid with one toss and raised his empty cup as a sign for more. He drank without speaking, never taking his eyes off the Apache subchief. Lacayuelo met the *blanco* chief's gaze and felt more than distrust. There was a challenge also. And he would try to drink his tizwin as rapidly.

Cline looked at the lieutenant anxiously. The scout was beginning to feel his drinks, and he'd had tizwin before.

"Mister, you'd better take it easy. This stuff'll do somethin' to you."

Towner sat erect with his legs crossed. "Mr. Cline, I may be young, but a long time ago my father taught me to drink like a gentleman. If I didn't think I could out-drink these creatures, I'd resign my commission."

"That's the trouble, they don't drink like gentlemen."

The lieutenant reached for the water bag again. "Play the game, Mr. Cline. Play the game." And oddly enough the words gave the scout confidence.

It was shortly after this that one of the Apaches screamed and leaped to his feet, drawing a knife from his breechclout. Five white men dropped their cups and raised pieces in one motion to cover the Apache who was about to leap over the mound of ashes. The sixth was doing quite another thing. He was laughing, and loud enough to make the Indian stop his motion in midair, so that one of his moccasins came down in the middle of the cook fire, the soft ashes puffing in a cloud of gray smoke. He jerked his foot up instinctively, but too quickly, so that he was thrown off balance back among the other Chiricahuas. Towner laughed all the louder.

Then he stopped abruptly and eyed the subchief coldly. He spoke slowly, carefully, to make certain the old Indian would understand.

"Lacayuelo, why do you bring boys to do the work of men? I have heard many tales of how brave the Apache warriors are, but now I see that these tales must surely be false. For what I have seen of the Apache makes me believe that he is an old woman or a very little boy. You do not sit like men of dignity and calmly drink your tizwin. You scream and jump and would commit murder if you had the chance. That is because your hearts are black. You do not have the hearts of true braves. I have come the distance of twenty sunsets to see the Apache because I have heard so many tales of wonder and bravery. And now I see that he cannot even drink a few cups of tizwin without turning into the desert dog. Surely this is not something a man can be proud of." He glanced at the scout. "Tell these other beasts what I said. I think Lacayuelo understood. Look at his face."

LACAYUELO LISTENED again as Cline repeated the words, and his face grew darker. As he rose to speak, his eyes were bleary from the tizwin, but he controlled his voice well, speaking slowly so that his thick tongue would not jumble the words.

"The *mejor* speaks as man much wiser than his years would have him be. You are young and I start to grow old and I can see what you are doing. Your words have stabbed our hearts. You tell us we are not men. I tell you, I know what you are doing. Still, we will sit and drink tizwin and by'n by I show you Chiricahua is more man than a *blanco*." He spoke gravely, solemnly. "You have called us many names. Now I will show you they are not true. Now you must show me that you are a man,

or I shall call you not only woman and little boy,
but dead fool!"

The men understood now, fully. It was a contest.
They were pitting their ability to drink against the
Apaches'. They understood well what would happen to the loser. And they understood that they re-
lied completely on the young Lieutenant Towner to
keep the Indians drinking. Occasionally, a man
would laugh to himself, *How the devil did I get
into this!* But it was a hollow laugh. For the most
part there was silence, a deathlike silence, for that's
what was in the air. It stretched from one line of
men over to the other and it held them transfixed.
This was the most serious drinking any trooper had
ever done—and it went on and on, into the dusk.

The Indians were becoming dim outlines in the
grayness when Towner ordered the fire. Lonnigan
worked cautiously, facing the Indians, though his
feet were very unsteady. He cursed with a thick
tongue the matches that kept going out in his fum-
bling fingers, but soon he had a good fire going.
Across the flames, Towner watched the shadows
dance on the faces of the Apaches. In the orange
light they were fierce, grotesque, black smudges
hiding eyes filmed and bulging with hate; but he
noticed other things too. Eyes that closed, opened,
then closed again for a longer time. A head would
nod. Soon one of the Apaches, without a sound, fell
back and lay motionless.

Within the next two hours, three more Indians slumped into unconsciousness. But not without continued prompting from the lieutenant. He drank his cupfuls down without hesitation, and when an Indian faltered for a minute, or would spill the liquid in his drunkenness, Towner was alert to sneer and goad him on to more.

Lacayuelo watched his strength melt away with the hot liquid, but he was powerless to do anything. At one time he began a chant, a song telling of all his warrior deeds; but the *blanco* chief howled with laughter. And when the Apache staggered to his feet to cross the fire, the lieutenant stopped laughing and stared at him silently. It was a look of contempt. A look that said, *I told you you were not a man.* And Lacayuelo fell back to show this insolent *muchacho* what a man really was. But it was becoming more difficult each hour.

The end was near. Lacayuelo knew it. His eyes moved up and down the line of his warriors. Only two were in sitting positions, but their heads drooped chin to chest. Neither had taken a drink in almost an hour. He looked across the dying fire. The scout lay belly-down on the hard ground, his arms outstretched unnaturally pointing in the direction of the three troopers, motionless on their backs. But the sergeant was still awake; head hanging, but awake. He would move slowly, the Indian thought. And the *blanco* chief still faced across the fire, his hat brim low masking his eyes. He could be asleep. . . .

The Indian swayed as he rose to his feet, leaned too far forward and fell to his hands and knees, tripping over the extended foot of one of the prostrate warriors. His head was clear, he could think, but his body would not react with the same accord. He stumbled as he rose again, this time shattering the pottery cup against a rock.

He looked quickly to the *blanco* chief. The form danced and swayed before his blurred vision, but that part which was the head did not move. The eyes still cloaked by the hat brim.

But now there was another motion. He stumbled forward kicking dirt into the dying fire and then stopped dead, swaying on feet spread slightly apart. He squinted hard to make the *blanco* chief stop swinging back and forth, and as the film fell away and the rotating motion slowed, he saw the revolving pistol pointed at his eyes. And through the piercing ring in his ears he heard the hammer click into cock position. It was all over.

Towner watched the old Indian sink to his knees slowly and then fall forward, rolling onto his side. He had the urge to pull the trigger, even though it was not necessary, even though it was all over. From across the glowing pile of ashes there was neither the sign of motion nor the hint of it.

He nudged Lonnigan who lifted his head momentarily, grunted, and then eased his thick body slowly backward until he was lying down. Like the others, he was past caring. Towner stumbled as he crossed the fire, his feet moving as if iron fetters were attached, but he shuffled on until he stood before Lacayuelo. He looked up and down the line of prostrate forms that revolved slowly on the ground, and then back at the subchief, shaking his head and blinking his eyes. All through the night his willpower had been using brute force to goad his body on, lashing the sinking feeling away with, *Show the savages!* Now it was over, and he could feel himself being drawn into the black nothingness of utter exhaustion. But there was one thing more to be done.

He bent over the still form of Lacayuelo and looked at his clothing closely, at the filthy jacket and ragged pants. Then the issue belt caught his eye. It was polished, gleaming. He unbuckled it and drew it off. The first thing he saw was the name on the inside—Byerlein. That was all. He drew his arm back and brought the barrel of the revolving pistol down upon the Indian's skull. And as he staggered down the line of unconscious figures, he brought the weapon down again and again against the heads of the Apaches. When it was finished, he felt better.

IT WAS FORTY miles back to Thomas. Forty blistering, dry miles through the furnace that was central

Arizona. Miles that cramped legs and jolted heads
already racked by the aftereffects of Apache corn
beer. And there were nine Chiricahua hostiles who
had to be watched, watched with a sharp eye;
though their feet were lashed beneath pony bellies
and their skulls throbbed with a brutal pain.

Just before sunset, the riders, caked with alkali
dust and heads bowed, rode across the parade at
Fort Thomas. Colonel Darck stepped to the front
of the ramada before his quarters to receive the
lieutenant who had wheeled off toward him.

"You lost some men, Lieutenant." The colonel
volunteered only this observation. It could mean
anything. His opinion would come later when
Towner made his official report. This meeting was
simply a courtesy. "You look all in, Mr. Towner.
Not used to the weather yet, eh? What do you say
to a whiskey before cleaning up?"

The colonel spoke about it for years after. Of
course he was polite about it, but it was the idea.
The young lieutenant was the only officer Darck
ever knew to refuse a whiskey punch after finishing
a blistering four-day patrol.

3

The Last Shot

FROM THE SHADE of the pines, looking across the draw, he watched the single file of cavalrymen come out of the timber onto the open bench. The first rider raised his arm and they moved at a slower pace down the slope, through the green-tinged brush. The sun made small flashes on the visors of their kepis and a clinking sound drifted faintly across the draw.

He had come down the same way a few minutes before and now he was certain that they would stay on his trail. Watching them, he sat his sorrel mare unmoving, his young face sun-darkened and clean-lined and glistening with perspiration, though the air was cool. A Sharps lay across his lap and he gripped it hard, then looked about quickly as if searching for a place to hide it. Instead he swung the stock against the sorrel's rump and guided her away from the rim, breaking into a run as they crossed a meadow of bear grass toward the darkness of a pine stand. And as he drew near, a rider, watching him closely, came out of the pines.

Lou Walker, the young man, swung his mount close to the other rider and pushed the rifle toward him.

"Give me your carbine, Risdon!"

"What happened?" the man said. Ed Risdon was close to fifty. He sat heavily in his saddle and his round, leathery face studied Walker calmly.

"I missed him."

"How could you miss? All you had to do was aim at his beard."

"His horse spooked as I fired. It reared up and I hit it in the withers."

"They see you?"

"I was up in the rocks and when I missed they took out after me. Give me the carbine. If I get caught they'll see it hasn't been fired."

"What if I get caught?" Risdon said.

"You won't if you scat."

Risdon drew the short rifle from its saddle scabbard and handed it to Lou Walker, exchanging it for Walker's Sharps. "Maybe," he said, "I'd better stay with you."

"Get home and tell Beckwith what happened—and get that gun out of here."

Risdon hesitated. "What'll I tell Barbara?"

Walker stared at him. "I don't like it any more than you do."

"I think maybe it's getting senseless," Risdon answered.

"Think what you want—just get the hell out of here."

Walker nudged the mare with his knee and rode away from Risdon, back toward the rim. As he neared it he looked around, across the meadow, to make certain Risdon was gone. He could hear the cavalrymen below him now, the clinking sound of their approach sharp in the crisp air, and waited until they could see him up through the trees before he started off, following the rim. There was a shout, then another, and when the carbine shot rang behind him he knew they had reached the crest. He swung from the high ground then, zigzagging down through the scattered piñons, guiding the reins loosely.

A quarter of the way from the bottom the dwarf pines gave up to brush and hard rock. Walker spurred toward the open slope, glancing over his shoulder, seeing the flashes of blue uniforms up through the trees. He heard the carbine report and the whine as the bullet glanced off rock. Then another. A third kicked up sand a few yards in front of the mare and she swerved suddenly on the slope. He tried to hold her in, but the mare was already side-slipping on the loose shale. Suddenly she was falling and Walker went out of the saddle. He tried to twist his body in the air—then he struck the slope and rolled. . . .

THERE WAS A stable smell of leather and damp horsehide. Again his body slammed against the ground and the shock of it brought open his eyes. They had carried him draped across a saddle and when they reached the others, a trooper threw his legs over the horse and he landed on his back.

He heard a voice say, "Sergeant!" close over him. He looked up and the trooper spat to the side. "He's awake."

Now there were other faces that looked down at him and they were all the same—shapeless kepis, tired, curious eyes, dirt in crease lines, and two- or three-day beards. Though there were some faces without the stubble, they were boys with the expressions of men. The blue uniforms were covered with fine dust and the jackets seemed ill-fitting, with buttons missing, and from the shoulders hung the oblong, leather-covered, wooden cases that hold seven cartridge tubes for a Spencer carbine.

And then another uniform was standing over him. Alkali dust made the Union blue seem faded, but the jacket held firmly to chest and shoulders and a full, red beard reached to the second button. The red beard moved.

"Mister, we owe you an apology, though I don't imagine it makes your head feel any better."

Walker relaxed slowly, sitting up, then came to his feet and stood in front of the red beard which was even with his own chin. But his leg buckled under him and he sat down again, feeling the stabbing in his right knee. He winced, but kept his eyes on the officer. He had imagined McGrail to be a much taller man and now he was surprised. *Stories make a man taller than he is. . . .* Then he felt better because Major McGrail was not unusually tall. Still, he was uneasy. Perhaps because he had tried to kill him not a half hour before.

"Your knee?" McGrail said.

Walker nodded, then said, "Where's my horse?"

"It was past saving."

"You didn't have a right to fire on me."

McGrail smiled faintly. "I'm told you had a damn uncommon guilty way of running when ordered to halt."

"I didn't hear anything."

"Perhaps you weren't listening."

"I don't wear a uniform."

"Did you ever?"

"Are you holding a trial?"

"Someone shooting at me arouses a fair amount of curiosity."

"So your men chased out and spotted me and thought I was the one."

McGrail said nothing. He extended his left hand to the side and the sergeant stepped quickly, placing in it the carbine he'd been holding.

McGrail handed the carbine to Walker. "We took the liberty of examining it," he said. "You see, the bullet struck my mount. From something with a large bore—a Sharps perhaps."

"And mine's a carbine that hasn't been fired."

"A Perry that hasn't been fired," McGrail corrected. "A Confederate make, isn't it?"

"As far as I know, this gun doesn't know north from south."

"I suppose not." McGrail smiled. "Which way are you going?" he said then.

"Valverde."

"Well, I can repay some inconvenience by offering you a remount home."

"I didn't say it was my home."

"In fact—" McGrail smiled "—you haven't said anything."

★ ★ ★

THE UNION CAVALRY Station, Valverde, New Mexico, was a mile north of the pueblo. McGrail swung his troop in that direction as they approached Valverde and Lou Walker sat his mount for some time watching the dust rise behind the line of cavalry. Then he went on—though the image of McGrail, red beard and tired eyes, remained in his mind.

Before reaching the plaza, he turned into a side street and tied the borrowed mount in front of a one-story adobe and went through the doorway that said EAT above it in large faded letters.

The man behind the bar looked up and nodded as he entered and the waiter, who was Mexican and wore a stained apron, also nodded. There were no patrons in the room, but Walker passed through it to a back room which was smaller and had only three tables. And as he sat down, the Mexican appeared in the doorway.

"You're limping."

"My horse threw me."

"That's a bad thing." The waiter considered this and then said, "What pleases you?"

"Brandy and coffee."

His knee was becoming stiff and was sensitive when he touched it. He rubbed it idly, becoming used to it, until the waiter returned and placed his tray on the table. The waiter poured coffee from a small porcelain pot, then raised the brandy bottle.

"In the coffee?"

He shook his head and watched as the waiter poured brandy into a glass. He looked up as a man came through the doorway.

Walker nodded and said, "Beckwith."

The man, in his mid-forties, was thin and he wore a heavy mustache that made his drawn face seem even narrower.

He said, "What's that?"

"Brandy."

"You better watch it." Sitting down, Beckwith's hand flicked against the waiter's arm. "We'll see you," he said and waited until the scuffing sound of the waiter's sandals had faded out of the room while he watched Walker closely.

"I saw McGrail ten minutes ago."

"I missed him."

"That's like telling me I've got eyes. All you had to do was aim at his beard."

"That's what Risdon said."

"Where is he?"

"He went back to del Norte."

"He was supposed to stay with you," Beckwith said.

"He went back to tell you what happened. I didn't know you were here."

"You don't seem too concerned about this."

"I'm tired," Walker said.

Beckwith stared at him without expression, coldly. "Listen," he said after a moment. "Every day that man stays alive, the Yankees get more to fight with. Not just beef and remounts, but recruits he sweet-talks into joining Sam Grant—" Beckwith paused.

"You've heard of a place called Five Forks—in Virginia?"

"Go on."

"A week ago Pickett got his pants beat off there. Fitz Lee's Cavalry was cut to pieces."

"Then it's nearly over," Walker said quietly.

"Hell no it ain't! Kirby Smith's still holding out in Mississippi. We got more land than just Virginia."

"And how many more lives?" Walker said.

"Quitting?"

"All of a sudden I'm tired." Beneath the table his hand rubbed the knee.

"Or is it scared?" Beckwith said.

"Leave me alone for a while."

"I asked you a question."

Walker's face hardened. "Where've you been for four years, Beckwith—del Norte? Or did you get over to Tascosa once. Tell me what you do to keep from getting scared?"

After a moment he said, "My knee's turning stiff."

"That's too bad," Beckwith said.

"Everything's too bad."

"You haven't answered me," Beckwith said. "What are you going to do?"

Walker drank off the brandy and dropped his arm heavily. "Kill him," he said finally.

★ ★ ★

HE TOOK A ROOM at the hotel and stretched out on the bed without removing his clothes, just his coat and boots. He hung his shoulder holster on the foot of the bed, but took out the handgun and placed it next to his leg; and he was asleep before he could think of the war or of Beckwith, the Confederate agent who'd never seen a skirmish, or McGrail, who had to be killed because he was a valuable Yankee officer. He did think of Barbara, Risdon's daughter, but it was only for a few minutes.

It was early morning when he awoke and before he opened his eyes he felt the stiffness in his knee. Without moving his leg he knew it was swollen: then, when he raised it, it began to throb.

It was the same leg a year ago. No, he thought now. Yellow Tavern was eleven months ago. He had been with a Texas Volunteer company assigned to Stuart's Cavalry. The defense of Richmond.

They could have stayed in the redoubts and waited, but that wasn't Stuart. He came out and threw his sabers in Sheridan's face at Yellow Tavern—straight on into the Whitworths the Yankees had captured and turned on them—and it wasn't enough. Sheridan wasn't McClellan. Walker remembered Stuart going down, shot through the lungs, and then his own mount was down and he was conscious only of the scalding pain in his right leg.

It was during his stay in the Richmond hospital that the civilian had come and asked him strange questions about how he thought about things, and finally began talking about soldiers without uniforms. "Spying?" he'd asked. Call it what you want, the civilian said. There's more than one way to fight a war.

They had picked him because he was a Texan, could speak some Spanish, and his war record was good. Three months later he was in Paso del Norte, with Beckwith's organization, buying guns for the Cause. Ed Risdon guided for them. Risdon had traded goods down through Chihuahua and Sonora for over fifteen years. He knew the country and he brought them through each time. About one trip a month.

His daughter, Barbara, waited in del Norte, watching for Lou Walker. Between trips they were together most of the time.

Then one day, that was two weeks ago, Beckwith told him what had to be done about McGrail. For only two troops of blue-bellies his command was doing a mountain of harm, getting men and supplies headed east safely. That would have to be stopped.

Beckwith is a strange man, he thought. He can become fanatical about the Cause, though he's never been east of the Panhandle. That's it, he thought now. That makes the difference. He didn't see the Wilderness, or Cold Harbor, or Yellow Tavern.

The morning wore on and he began to feel hungry, but his body ached and he remained on the bed, smoking cigarettes when it would occur to him, not moving his leg. He wasn't worried about the knee.

He was dozing again when the light knocks sounded on the door and he sat upright with the suddenness of it and winced, feeling the muscles pull in his knee.

"Who is it?" His palm covered the bone handle of the pistol next to him.

A girl's voice answered him.

★ ★ ★

HE WAS OFF the bed, went to the door, opened it, and the girl was in his arms. Close to her cheek he said, "Barbara—" but her mouth brushed against his and that was all he said. For a moment they clung together, then he drew her inside and closed the door.

"How'd you find me?"

"Beckwith told us."

"Your father's with you?"

She nodded. Her dark hair was pulled back tightly into a chignon and it made her face seem delicately small. "I told him I wanted to be with you."

"That must have touched him," Walker said. He led her to the bed and sat down next to her. There was no chair in the room and he felt suddenly embarrassed at being alone with her, and at the same time he was conscious of his uncombed hair and the two-day beard, even though he knew it would not matter to her.

"Lou, you hurt your leg!"

Her gaze remained on his knee, but she said, "You're going to try again, aren't you?"

"You're not supposed to know about that."

Her eyes lifted to his, frowning. "What good will it do?"

"If I knew all the whys, I'd be wearing yellow epaulettes with fringe."

"One more dead man isn't going to help anything."

"You didn't talk to Beckwith very long."

For a moment the girl was silent. "We're leaving," she said then.

"For where?"

"I don't know—toward California."

"Your dad's idea?"

"Partly. But maybe I'm more worn out than he is." She looked at him longingly. "Lou—come with us."

"You know better than that."

"Why?"

"I'd be a deserter."

Her eyes begged him again, but she said nothing and finally her head lowered and she stared at her hands in her lap. Walker made a cigarette and smoked it in the silence, trying to rationalize going with them: but he could not.

The girl was rising when they heard the footsteps outside the door. Then the three knocks.

"Walker?" Beckwith's voice came from the hall.

Walker looked at the girl, then went to the door and opened it. Risdon stood in the doorway. Behind him, Beckwith said, "Go on," and Risdon moved into the room. Beckwith followed a step behind, with the barrel of his pistol pressed into the man's back.

Beckwith looked at the girl and then to Walker. "Lou," he said. "You're about the most resourceful man I know, even when you're sick."

The girl had gone to her father and now she looked at him with frightened surprise. "You told him!"

"I had to. I don't want him saying we're running away."

"What do you call it?" Beckwith said.

"I'm getting too old to play soldierboy," Risdon said.

"You think you can just walk away?"

"He's not in the army," Walker said now. "He can leave any time he feels like it!"

"With all he knows about us?" Beckwith asked.

"God, if you can't trust him, who can you!"

"Lou, I wonder about that more and more every day."

"Cut out the foolishness!"

"Were you going, too?"

"No."

"Just take your word for it?" Beckwith's thin face was expressionless. "Lou," he said, "I'm not play-actin'. You know what they do to deserters."

"What's he deserting from?"

"Me," Beckwith said quietly. He added, then, "Lou, I'll have to take your word about you not go-

ing—but get over on the bed out of the way." Walker
hesitated and Beckwith turned the pistol on him
threateningly. "I can include you as easily as not."

Walker backed against the bed and eased down,
keeping his right leg stiffly in front of him. As he
sank to the bed, something hard dug against his
thigh. His hand moved to the side of his leg, then
stopped. It was his pistol.

Risdon was watching his daughter and now he
was about to speak: it was on his face.

"Keep it to yourself," Beckwith said to him. "I
don't want to hear any more."

"What are you going to do?" Walker asked him
quietly. His hand was on the pistol butt now, close
under his leg.

"What I have to," Beckwith said. "We can't take
chances on either of them."

"Here?"

"Out somewhere."

Walker's fingers closed around the pistol grip. He
hesitated, because he wanted to do this the right
way, and he wasn't sure what that was. He heard
Risdon say, "Beckwith—" and saw the agent's head
turn toward Risdon. At that moment, Walker
raised the pistol and cocked it.

Beckwith heard the click and his head swung
back. He looked at Walker as if what he saw could
not be possible.

Walker held the pistol dead on the agent's chest.

"I'm not going to try to convince you of anything," he said. "Just let go of the gun."

The surprise passed and Beckwith's drawn face scowled. "You're making the biggest mistake of your life."

"If you don't think I'd shoot, hold on to that gun for three more seconds."

Beckwith's pistol was pointed midway between Risdon and Walker. His eyes held on Walker's face, trying to read something there. Then, slowly, his arm lowered and when his hand reached his side, the fingers opened and the pistol dropped to the floor.

Risdon stooped, picked it up and glanced at Beckwith as he rose.

"You just lost yourself a job."

"You've got to take him with you," Walker said now. "Drop him at maybe Cuchillo—by the time he finds help you'll have all the distance you'd need."

Risdon frowned. "You're coming now, aren't you?"

Walker shook his head.

The girl looked at him in disbelief. "Lou, why would you stay now?"

"The same reason as before."

"But it's different now!"

"Why is it? I'm still a soldier. I haven't been serving under a private flag of Beckwith's."

The girl continued to look at him with the plea in her eyes, but now there was nothing she could say.

Risdon shrugged. "Well, you can't fight that."

Walker pulled on his boots, then lifted the shoulder holster from the bedpost and slipped his arm through it and inserted the handgun. He picked up his coat and moved to the girl.

"If you don't understand," he said quietly, "then I don't know what I can say."

She looked up into his face, but without smiling, and then she kissed him.

Risdon said, "She's tryin'." His eyes followed Walker moving to the door. "Lou," he said. "We thought we'd follow the Rio Grande to Cuchillo then bear west toward Santa Rita."

Unexpectedly, Walker smiled, but he said nothing going out the door.

AT YELLOW TAVERN he had killed a Union soldier. Perhaps he had killed others, but the one at Yellow Tavern was the only one he was sure of. It had been at close range, firing down into the soldier's face as the Yankee's bayonet thrust caught in his horse's mane. He fired and the blue uniform disappeared. That simple. What he was about to do no longer seemed a part of war, because the man had a name and was not just a blue uniform.

He rode out from Valverde to the cavalry station at a walk, moving the borrowed mount unhurriedly, his right leg hanging out of the stirrup. Nearing the adobes a trooper rode by and shouted, but the sound of his running mount covered the words.

The sunlight on the gray adobe was cold, because there was no one about and there were no sounds. Over the row of bare houses, far to the north, reaching into the clouds, was the whiteness of Sangre de Cristo. This, too, caused the cavalry station to seem drab. Walker knew a patrol was out. Perhaps McGrail had taken it. For a moment he felt relief, but knew that would solve nothing.

He went through a doorway above which a wooden shingle read: HEADQUARTERS—VALVERDE STATION—COS, D & E—9TH US CAVALRY.

At the desk a sergeant looked up and momentarily there was recognition on his face. But he said nothing, he only listened to the name that was given him, then stepped into the next room and closed the door behind him.

He reappeared almost immediately. "The major will see you," and stepped aside to let Walker pass.

McGrail's back was turned. He stood at the window behind his desk, looking out at the sand and glare.

He did not turn, but when the door closed, he said, "I've been expecting you."

Walker hesitated. "Why?"

McGrail turned then. He was holding a revolving pistol in his right hand, and with the other he was wiping a cloth along the barrel.

"To return the horse you borrowed," he said. "Why else?"

Walker was silent. The surprise was on his face for a brief moment. It passed, and still he did not say anything.

"How's the leg?"

"Stiff."

"I suppose it would be."

McGrail moved the cloth slowly, steadily along the pistol barrel. Abruptly he said, "You wouldn't know the whereabouts of a man named Beckwith, would you?"

Walker was startled. "Should I?"

"You're not one for answering questions, are you?"

Walker unbuttoned his coat and drew tobacco from his shirt. He made a cigarette and replaced the tobacco, leaving his coat open.

"I could never wear a shoulder holster," McGrail said. "Would always feel bound."

Walker exhaled cigarette smoke. "You get used to anything."

"I thought you might have heard of this Beckwith," McGrail said. "I'm rather anxious to meet him, myself—you see, he's a Confederate agent."

"Why are you telling me that?"

McGrail shrugged. "Just conversation. Thought you might be interested. You see, this Beckwith thinks he's been putting something over on us, but there are as many people in Valverde giving information to me as there are to him." McGrail was relaxed. His eyes were not tired now, and his full red beard had been combed and trimmed.

"People like waiters and bartenders?" Walker said.

"All kinds of people, doing their bit." McGrail smiled.

Walker dropped his cigarette to the plank flooring and stepped on it and saw the major frown. "If you have something to say, say it."

McGrail hesitated, watching Walker closely. He had been leaning against the front of his desk. Now he moved around it and, next to the window, unrolled a wall map by pulling a short cord. He beckoned to Walker with the handgun.

He moved forward hesitantly and watched McGrail point with his left hand to a dot on the map, but he could not read the name because of McGrail's hand. But east and north of the dot there were other names that could be read. Five Forks, Malvern Hill, Seven Pines. And suddenly he felt the skin prickle on the nape of his neck and between his shoulders.

"We heard less than an hour ago," McGrail said quietly. "On the morning of April ninth, here at Appomattox, Lee surrendered to General Grant. Mr. Walker, the war is over."

The room was silent. Walker's eyes remained on the map, unmoving. *The war's over*, he said in his mind, and repeated the words. *The war's over*. He felt relief. He waited for something else, but that was all. He felt only relief. *How are you supposed to feel when you lose a war?* he thought. He looked at McGrail now and watched the cavalryman step to his desk and lay his pistol there. He felt his own pistol, heavy beneath his left arm, and now his hand dropped slowly from his coat front.

"I just now sent a man to Valverde," McGrail said. "You must have passed him. News travels slowly out here, doesn't it?" he said now. "You know April the ninth was two days ago—the day before we found you in that draw."

The cavalryman began arranging papers that were scattered over the polished surface of his desk. He looked up at Walker who was staring at him strangely.

"Mr. Walker, if you'll excuse me, I've a mountain of reports to wade through that have to be done today. That was all you wanted, wasn't it? To return the horse?"

Walker hesitated. "As a matter of fact, there was something else."

McGrail looked up again. "Yes?"

"I wondered if you might have a rig I could buy," Walker said. A grin was forming through the beard stubble. "It's hard going astride, with one leg dragging. You see, I've got a long way to go—down the Rio Grande to Cuchillo, then west toward Santa Rita—"

4

Blood Money

THE YUMA SAVINGS and Loan, Asunción Branch, was held up on a Monday morning, early. By eight o'clock the doctor had dug the bullet out of Elton Goss's middle and said if he lived, then you didn't need doctors anymore—the age of miracles was back. By nine Freehouser, the Asunción marshal, had all the facts—even the identity of the five holdup men—thanks to the Centralia Hotel night clerk's having been awake to see four of them come down from their rooms just after sunup. Then, he had tried to make the faces register in his mind, but even squinting and wrinkling his forehead did no good. The fifth man had been in the hotel lobby most of the night and the clerk knew for sure who he was, but didn't at the time associate him with the others.

Later, when Freehouser showed him the WANTED dodgers, then he was dead sure about all of them.

Four were desperadoes. Well known, though with beard bristles and range clothes they looked like anybody else. First, the Harlan brothers, Ford and Eugene. Ford was boss: Eugene was too lazy to work. Then Deke, an old hand whose real name was something Deacon, though no one knew what for sure. And the fourth, Sonny Navarez, wanted in Sonora by the rurales; in Arizona, by the marshal's office. He, like the others, had served time in the territorial prison at Yuma.

As far as Freehouser was concerned, they weren't going back to Yuma if he caught them. Not with Elton Goss dying and his dad yelling for blood.

The fifth outlaw was identified as Rich Miller, a rider from down by Four Tanks. Those who knew of him said he was weathered good for his age, though not as tough as he thought he was. A boy going on eighteen and getting funny ideas in his brain because of the changing chemistry in his body. The bartender at the Centralia said Rich had been in and out all day, looking like he was mad at somebody. So they judged Rich had gotten drunk and was talked into something that was way over his head.

A hand from F-T Connected, which was out of Four Tanks, said Rich Miller'd been let go the day before, when the old man caught him drunk up at a line shack and not tending his fences. So what the Centralia bartender said was probably true. Freehouser said it was just too damn bad for him, that's all.

Monday afternoon the marshal's posse was in Four Tanks, then heading east toward the jagged andesite peaks of the Kofas. McKelway, the law at Four Tanks, had joined the posse, bringing five men with him, and offering a neighborly hand. But he became hard-to-hold eager when he found out who they were after. The Fords, Deke, and Navarez had dead-or-alive money on them. McKelway knew Rich Miller and said he just ought to have his nose wiped and run off home. But Freehouser looked at it differently.

This was armed robbery. Goss, the bank manager, and his son Elton, who clerked for him, were hauled out of bed by two men—they turned out to be Eugene Harlan and Deke. Ford Harlan and Sonny Navarez were waiting at the rear door of the bank. The robbery would have come off without incident if Elton hadn't gone for a gun in a desk drawer. The elder Goss wasn't sure which one shot him. Then they were gone, with twelve thousand dollars.

They rode around front and Rich Miller came out of the Centralia to join them. He'd been sitting at the window, asleep, the clerk thought, wearing off a drunk. He was used to having riders do that.

When the rooms were filled up he didn't care. But Rich Miller suddenly came alive and swung onto a mount the Mexican was leading. So all that time he must have been watching the front to see no one sneaked up on them.

McKelway said a boy ought to be allowed one big mistake before he was called hard on something he'd done. Besides, Rich Miller's name didn't bring any reward money.

Tuesday morning, the twenty-man posse was deep in the Kofas. Gray rock towering on all sides, wild country, and now, no trail. Freehouser decided they would split up, climb to higher ground, and wait. Just look around. He sent a man back to Four Tanks to wire Yuma and Aztec in case the outlaws got through the Kofas. But Freehouser was sure they were still in the mountains, somewhere.

Wednesday morning his hunch paid off. One of McKelway's men spotted a rider, and the posse closed in by means of a mirror-flash system they'd planned beforehand. The rider turned out to be Ford Harlan.

Wednesday afternoon Ford Harlan was dead.

He had led them a chase most of the morning, slipping through the man net, but near noon he turned into a dead-end canyon, a deserted mine site that once had been Sweet Mary No. 1. Ford Harlan had been urging his mount up a slope above the mine works, toward an adobe hut perched on a

ledge about three hundred yards up, when Freehouser cupped his hands and called for him to halt.
He kept on. A moment later Jim Mission, McKelway's deputy, knocked him out of the saddle with a
single shot from his Remington.

Then McKelway and Mission volunteered to
bring Ford Harlan down. McKelway tied a white
neckerchief to the end of his Sharps for a truce flag
and they went up. Freehouser had said if you want
to get Ford, you might as well go a few more steps
and ask the rest if they want to give up. They were
almost to the body when the pistol fire broke from
above. They scrambled down fast and when they
reached the posse, Freehouser was smiling.

They were all up there, Eugene and Deke and the
Mexican and Rich Miller. One of them had lost his
nerve and opened up. You could see it on Freehouser's face. The self-satisfaction. They were
trapped in an old assay shack with a sheer sandstone wall towering behind it—thin shadow lines of
crevices reaching to slender pinnacles—and only
one way to come down. The original mine opening
was on the same shelf; probably they'd hid their
horses there.

Freehouser was a contented man; he had all the
time in the world to figure how to pry them out of
the 'dobe. He even listened to McKelway and admitted that maybe the kid, Rich Miller, shouldn't
be hung with the others—if he didn't get shot first.

Some of the posse went back home, because they had jobs to hold down, but the next day, others came out from Asunción and Four Tanks to see the fun.

IT SEEMED NATURAL that Deke should take over as boss. There was no discussing it; no one gave it a thought. Ford was dead. Eugene was indifferent. Sonny Navarez was Mexican, and Rich Miller was a kid.

The boy had wondered why Deke wasn't the boss even before. Maybe Deke didn't have Ford's nerve, but he had it over him in age and learning. Still, a man gets old and he thinks of too many what-ifs. And sometimes Deke was scary the way he talked about fate and God pulling little strings to steer men around where they didn't want to go.

He was at the window on the right side of the doorway, which was open because there was no door. Eugene and Deke were at the left front window. He could hear Sonny Navarez behind him moving gear around, but the boy did not take his eyes from the slope.

Deke lounged against the wall, his face close to the window frame, his carbine balanced on the sill. Eugene was a step behind him. He was a heavy-boned man, shoulders stretching his shirt tight, and tall, though Deke was taller when he wasn't lounging. Eugene pulled at his shirt, sticking to his body with perspiration. The sun was straight overhead and the heat pushed into the canyon without first being deflected by the rimrock.

The Mexican drew his carbine from his bedroll and moved up next to Rich Miller, and now the four of them were looking down the slope, all thinking pretty much the same thing, though in different ways.

Eugene Harlan broke the silence. "I shouldn't of fired at them."

It could have gone unsaid. Deke shrugged. "That's under the bridge."

"I wasn't thinking."

Deke did not bother to look at him. "Well, you better start."

"It wasn't my fault. Ford led 'em here!"

"Nobody's blaming you for anything. They'd a got us anyway, sooner or later. It was on the wall."

Eugene was silent, and then he said, "What happens if we give ourselves up?"

Deke glanced at him now. "What do you think?"

Sonny Navarez grinned. "I think they would invite us to the rope dance."

"Ford's the one shot that boy in the bank," Eugene protested. "They already got him."

"How would they know he's the one?" Deke said.

"We'll tell them."

Deke shook his head. "Get a drink and you'll be doing your nerves a favor."

Sonny Navarez and Rich Miller looked at Deke and both of them grinned, but they said nothing and after a moment they looked away again, down the slope, which fell smooth and steep. Slightly to the left, beyond an ore tailing, rose the weathered gray scaffolding over the main shaft; below it, the rickety structure of the crushing mill and, past that, six rusted tanks cradled in a framework of decaying timber. These were roughly three hundred yards down the slope. There was another hundred to the clapboard company buildings straggled along the base of the far slope.

A sign hanging from the veranda of the largest building said SWEET MARY NO. 1—EL TESORERO MINING CO.—FOUR TANKS, ARIZONA TERR. Most of the possemen now sat in the shade of this building.

Deke raised his hat again and passed a hand over his bald head, then down over his face, weathered and beard stubbled, contrasting with the delicate whiteness of his skull. Rich Miller's eyes came back up the slope, hesitating on Ford Harlan's facedown body. Then he removed his hat, passed a sleeve across his forehead, and replaced the curled brim low over his eyes.

He heard Eugene say, "You can't tell what they'll do."

"They won't send us back to Yuma," Deke said. "That's one thing you can count on. And it costs money to rig a gallows. They'd just as lief do it here, with a gun—appeals to the sporting blood."

Sonny Navarez said, "I once shot a mountain sheep in this same canyon that weighed as much as a man."

"Right from the start there were signs," Deke said. "I was a fool not to heed them. Now it's too late. Something's brought us to die here all together, and we can't escape it. You can't escape your doom."

Sonny Navarez said, "I think it was twelve thousand dollars that brought us."

"Sure it was the money, in a way," Deke said. "But we're so busy listening to Ford tell how easy money's restin' in the bank, waitin' to be sent to Yuma, we're not seein' the signs. Things that've never happened before. Like Ford insisting we got to have five—so he picks up this kid—"

Rich Miller said, "Wait a minute!" because it didn't sound right.

Deke held up his hand. "I'm talking about the signs—and Ford all of a sudden gettin' the urge to go on scout when he never done anything like that before. It was all working toward this—and now there's nothing we can do about it."

"I ain't going to get shot up just because you got a crazy notion," Eugene said.

Deke shook his head, wearily. "It's sealed up now. After fate shows how it's going, then it's too late."

"I didn't shoot that man in the bank!"

"You think they'll bother to ask you?"

"Damn it, I'll tell 'em—and they'll have to prove I did it!"

"If you can get close enough to 'em without gettin' shot," Deke said quietly. He brought out field glasses from his saddlebags, which were below the window, and put the glasses to his face, edging them along the men far below in front of the company buildings.

Rich Miller said to him, "What do you see down there?"

"Same thing you do, only bigger."

"I think," Sonny Navarez said to Deke, "that you are right in what you have said, that they will try hard to kill us—but this boy is not one of us. I think if he would surrender, they would not kill him. Prison, perhaps, but prison is better than dying."

"You worry about yourself," Rich Miller said.

"The time to be brave," the Mexican said, "is when they are handing out medals."

"You heard him," Deke said. "Worry about your own hide. The more people we got, the longer we last. There's nothing that says if you're going to get killed, you got to hurry it up."

Rich Miller watched Eugene move back to the table along the rear wall and pick up the whiskey bottle that was there. The boy passed his tongue over dry lips, watching Eugene drink. It would be good to have a drink, he thought. No, it wouldn't. It would be bad. You drank too much and that's

why you're here. That's why you're going to get
shot or hung.

But he could not sincerely believe what Deke had
said. That one way of the other, this was the end.
Down the slope the posse was very far away—dots
of men that seemed too small to be a threat. He did
not feel sorry about joining the holdup, because he
did not let himself think about it. He did feel something resembling sorry for the man in the bank. But
he shouldn't have reached for the gun. I wonder if I
would have, he thought.

It wasn't so bad up here in the 'dobe. Plenty of
water and grub. Maybe we'll have some fun. Look
at that crazy Mexican, talking about hunting
mountain sheep.

If you were in jail you could say, all right, you
made a mistake; but how do you know if you've
made a mistake when you're still alive and got two
thousand dollars in your pants? My God, a man can
do just about anything with two thousand dollars!

FREEHOUSER SAT in the shade, not saying anything.
McKelway came to him, biting on his pipe idly, and
after a while pointed to the mine-shaft scaffolding
and said how a man with a good rifle might be able
to draw a bead and throw something in that open
doorway if he was sitting way up there on top.

Freehouser studied the ore tailings, furrowed and steep, that extended out from the slope on both sides of the hut. If a man was going up to that 'dobe, he'd have to go straight up, right into their guns. Maybe McKelway had something. Soften them up a bit.

STANDING BY the windows, watching the possemen not moving, became tiresome. So one by one they would go back to the table and take a drink. Rich Miller took his turn and it tasted good. But he did not drink much.

Still, the time dragged on—until Eugene thought of something. He went to his gear and drew a deck of cards.

Sonny Navarez said, "I have not played often."

"Stand by the window awhile," Deke told him. "Then somebody'll spell you. You got enough cash to learn with."

Eugene shook his head, thinking of his brother, who had taken twice as much as the others because the holdup had been his idea. "Damn Ford had four thousand in his bags. . . ."

They started playing, using matches for chips, each one worth a dollar. Rich Miller said the stakes were big . . . he'd never played higher than nickel-dime before; but he began winning right off and he changed his tune. Most of the time they played five-card stud. Deke said it separated the men from the boys and he looked at Rich Miller when he said it. Deke played with a dumb face, but would smile after the last card was dealt—as if the last card always twinned the one he had in the hole. And he lost every hand. Eugene and Rich Miller took turns winning the pots, and after a while Deke stopped smiling.

"We're raising the stakes," he said finally. "Each stick's worth ten dollars." Deke's cut was down to a few hundred dollars.

Eugene took a drink and wiped his mouth and grinned. "Ain't you losing it fast enough?"

Rich Miller grinned with him.

Deke said, "Just deal the cards."

McKelway reached the platform on top of the shaft scaffolding and dropped the line to haul up the rifles—his own Sharps and Jim Mission's roll-block Remington. He was glad Jim Mission was coming up with him. Jim was company and could shoot probably better than he could.

When Jim reached the platform the two men nodded and smiled, then loaded their rifles and practice-sighted on the doorway. McKelway said, Try not to hit the boy, though knocking off any of the others would be doing mankind a good turn, and Jim Mission said it was all right with him.

EUGENE GOT UP from the table unsteadily, tipping back his chair; he was grinning and stuffing currency into his pants pockets. In two hours he had won every cent of Deke's and Rich Miller's money. They remained seated, watching him sullenly, thinking it was a damn fool thing to try and win back all your losings in a couple of hands. Eugene took another pull at the bottle and wiped his mouth and looked at them, but he only grinned.

"Sonny!" He called to the Mexican lounging beside the window. "Your turn to get skinned."

The Mexican shook his head. "I could not oppose such luck."

"Come on!"

Sonny Navarez shook his head again and smiled.

Harlan looked at him steadily, frowning. "Are you going to play?"

"Why should I give you my money?"

"You don't come over here, I'll come get you."

The Mexican did not smile now and the room was silent. Rich Miller started to rise, but Deke was up first. "Gene, you want to fight somebody—there's plenty outside."

Eugene ignored him and kept on toward Sonny.

The Mexican's hand edged toward his holstered pistol.

"Gene, you sit down now," Deke said tensely.

Eugene stepped into the rectangle of sunlight carpeting in from the doorway. He was stepping out of it when the rifle cracked and sang in the open stillness. Eugene's hands clawed at his face and he dropped without uttering a sound.

* * *

McKELWAY RELOADED quickly. He had got one of them, he was sure of that. And it hadn't looked like the boy, else he wouldn't have fired. Jim Mission told him it was good shooting. After that McKelway did some figuring.

From the crest of the ore tailing in front of them, they'd be only about fifty yards from the hut. The only trouble was, they'd be out in the open. He told Jim Mission about it and he said why not go up after dark; then if they didn't see anything they'd still be close enough to shoot at sounds. McKelway said he was just waiting for Jim to say it.

* * *

THERE WAS NO poker the rest of the afternoon. Deke had dragged Eugene by his boots out of the doorway and placed him against a side wall with his hands on his chest, not crossed, but pushed inside his coat. He took the money out of Eugene's pockets—six thousand dollars—and laid it on the table. Then he sat down and looked at it.

Rich Miller pressed close to the wall by the window, studying the slope, wondering where the man with the rifle was. His eyes hung on the weathered shaft scaffolding, and now he wasn't so sure if there'd be any fun.

Once Deke said, "Now it's starting to show itself," but they didn't bother to ask him what.

Sonny Navarez stayed by a window. He would look at Eugene's body, but most of the time he was watching the dying sun. Rich Miller noticed this, but he figured the Mexican was thinking about God—or heaven or hell—because there was a dead man in the room. Sonny had crossed himself when Eugene was cut down, even though he would have killed him himself a minute before.

The sun was below the canyon rim, though the sky still reflected it red and orange, when Sonny Navarez pulled his pistol.

Deke was raising the bottle. He glanced at the Mexican, but only momentarily. He took a long swallow then and extended the bottle to Rich Miller. But the boy was staring at Sonny Navarez. Deke's head turned abruptly. Sonny's long-barreled .44 was pointing toward them.

Deke took his time putting down the bottle. He looked up again. "What's the idea?"

The Mexican said, "When it is dark I'm leaving."

Deke nodded to the pistol. "You think we're going to try and stop you?"

"You might. I am taking the money."

"You're wasting your time."

Sonny Navarez shrugged. "*Qué va*—it's worth a try. From no matter where you die, it's the same distance to hell."

"You wouldn't have a chance," Rich Miller said. "There's somebody out there close with a rifle dead on this place."

"For this money a man will brave many things," the Mexican said. "And—I am not leaving until dark." Then he told them to face the wall, and when they did, he picked up the bundles of oversize bills and stuffed them inside his jacket.

Rich Miller said, "Do you think you'll get through?"

"Probably no."

Deke said, "You're a damn fool."

"If I get out," Sonny Navarez said, "I will visit a priest and give his church part of the money, and not rob again."

"It's too late for that," Deke said. "It's too late for anything."

"No," the Mexican insisted. "I will be very sorry for this crime. With the money that is left after the church I will buy my mother a house in Hermosillo and after that I will recite the rosary every day."

Deke shook his head. "Things are going the way

they are for a reason we don't know. But nothing you can do will change it."

The Mexican shrugged and said, "*Qué va—*"

It was almost full dark when Sonny Navarez moved to the doorway. He stood next to the opening and holstered his pistol and lifted his carbine, which was there against the wall. He levered a shell into the breech and stepped into the opening, crouching slightly. He hesitated, as if listening, then turned to the two men at the table and nodded. As he was turning back, the rifle shot rang in the dim stillness and echoed up-canyon. Sonny Navarez doubled, sinking to his knees, and hung there momentarily, as if in prayer, before falling half through the doorway.

* * *

LATER, McKELWAY and Mission climbed down from the ore tailing and reported to Freehouser. The marshal said three out of five men wasn't bad for one day's work. They were sitting on the porch, cigarettes glowing in the darkness, when the rider came in from Asunción. He told them that Elton Goss was going to pull through.

Freehouser laughed and said, well, he guessed the age of miracles was back. A good one on the doctor, eh?

The news made everybody feel pretty good, because Elton was a nice boy. McKelway mentioned that it would also make it a whole lot easier on Rich Miller.

LOOKING OUT into the night, the boy could just barely make out the shapes of the mine structures and the cyanide vats, which Deke had told him held 250 tons of ore and had to be hauled all the way across the desert from Yuma. How did he say it? The ore'd pour into the crusher—jaws and rollers that'd beat it almost to powder—then pass into the vats and get leached in cyanide for nine days. Five pounds of cyanide to the ton of water, that was it. He thought, *What's the sense in remembering that?*

It's a strange thing, Rich Miller thought now, *how in two days a man can change from a thirty-a-month rider to an outlaw and not even feel it. Almost like the man has nothing to do with it. Just a rope pulling you into things.*

He remembered earlier in the day, being eager, looking forward to doing some long-range shooting, but seeing the situation apart from himself. He wondered how he could have thought this. Now there were two dead men in the room—that was the difference.

Later on, he got to thinking about Eugene breaking the poker game and about the Mexican. It occurred to him that both of them, for a short space of time, had all of the money, and now they were dead. Ford had taken the biggest cut, and he was dead. Toward morning he dozed and when he awoke, Deke was sitting, leaning against the wall below the other window.

Deke was silent and Rich Miller said, for something to say, "When they going to try for us?"

"When they get good and damn ready."

Rich Miller was silent and after a while he said, "We could take a chance and give up—you know, not like surrenderin'—with the idea of gettin' away later on when they ain't a hundred of 'em around."

"You know what I told you."

"But you ain't dead sure about that."

"I'd say I'm a little older than you are."

Rich Miller did not answer. Damn, he hated for someone to tell him that. As if old men naturally knew more than young ones. Taking credit for being older when they didn't have anything to do with it.

"What're you thinking about?" Deke said.

"Giving up."

Deke exhaled slowly. "You saw what happens if you go through that door."

"There's other ways."

"Like what?"

"Wavin' a flag."

"You wave anything out that door," Deke said quietly, "I'll kill you."

✯   ✯   ✯

HE'S CRAZY, RICH thought. *He's honest-to-God crazy and doesn't know it.* Deke had butted the table against the wall under the window and now they sat opposite each other, Deke on one side of the window, the boy on the other. Deke had divided the eight thousand dollars between them and said they were going to play poker to keep their minds from blowing away. He placed his pistol on the edge of the table.

They stayed fairly close at first, each winning about the same number of pots, but after a while the boy began to win more often. In the quietness he thought of many things—like not being able to give himself up—and then he remembered something which had occurred to him earlier.

"Deke," the boy said, "you know why Sonny and Eugene got killed?"

"I've been telling you why. 'Cause they were destined to."

"But why?"

"No one knows that."

"I do." The boy watched the older man closely. "Because they had the money." He paused. "Ford had most of it, and he was the first. Eugene had all but Sonny's when he got hit. Then Sonny took all of it and he lasted less than an hour."

Deke said nothing, but his sunken expression seemed more drawn.

They played on in silence and slowly Rich Miller was taking more and more of the money. Deke seemed uncomfortable and he said quietly that he guessed it just wasn't his day. In less than an hour he was down to two hundred and fifty dollars.

"You might clean me out," Deke said.

Rich Miller said nothing and dealt the cards. The first ones down, then a queen to Deke and a jack to himself. He looked at his hole card. A ten of diamonds. Deke bet fifty dollars on the queen.

"You must have twin girls," the boy said.

"You know how to find out."

Rich Miller's next card was a king. Deke's an ace. He bet fifty dollars again. Their fourth cards were low and no help, but Deke pushed in all the money he had.

"That's on a hunch," he said.

Rich Miller dealt the last cards—a queen to Deke, making it an ace, a five, and two queens. He gave himself a second king.

"What you show beats me," Deke said, grinning. He pushed away from the table and stood up. "You got it all, boy. You know what that means."

"It means I'm giving up."

"It's too late. You explained it yourself a while ago—the man who gets the money gets killed!" Deke was grinning deeply. "Now I don't have anything."

"You're dead sure you'll be last."

"As sure as a man can be. It's the handwriting."

"What good'll it do you?"

"Who knows?"

"You're so dead sure, go stand in that doorway." Deke was silent.

"What about your handwritin'? The pattern says you'll be the last, and even then, who knows? That all the bunk?"

Deke hesitated momentarily, then walked slowly toward the doorway. He stopped next to it, stiffly. Then he moved out.

Rich Miller's eyes stayed on Deke as his hand moved across the table. He lifted Deke's pistol from the table edge and swung it out the window and fired in the direction of the scaffolding.

A high-pitched, whining report answered the shot and hung longer in the air. Deke staggered, turning back into the room, and had time to look at the boy in wide-eyed amazement. Then he was dead.

The boy returned to the window after getting his carbine and, with his bandanna tied to the end of the barrel, waved it in a slow arc back and forth. Once they started up the slope he sat back in the chair and idly turned over his hole card, the ten.

The possemen were drawing closer, up to Ford

Harlan's body now. He flipped Deke's hole card. It landed on top of the two queens. Three ladies.

He rose and moved to the doorway as he saw the men nearing the shelf, then glanced down at Deke and shook his head. I sure am crazy, he thought. I never heard before of a man cheating to lose.

He walked through the doorway with his hands above his head.

5

Saint with a Six-Gun

INSIDE THE HOTEL café, Lyall Quinlan sat at the counter having his breakfast. Every once in a while he would look over at Elodie Wells. Elodie had served him, but now her back was to him; she was looking out the big window over the lower part that was green painted and said REGENT CAFÉ in white—looking across the street to the Tularosa jail. Horses and wagons were hitched there and down the street both ways, and behind the jailhouse in the big yard where everybody was now, that's where they were hanging Bobby Valdez.

Out on the street there wasn't a sound. Inside now, just the noise of Lyall Quinlan's palm popping the bottom of the ketchup bottle until it flowed out over his eggs. Elodie scowled at him as if she was trying to hear something and Lyall was interrupting the best part. Lyall just smiled at her, a young-kid smile, and began eating his eggs. Elodie, like about everybody in Tularosa, had been excited all week long waiting for this day to come—a whole week while Bobby Valdez sat in his cell with Lyall Quinlan guarding him. Elodie was mad because she had to work this morning. Lyall felt pretty good, so he just went on eating his eggs. . . .

BOHANNON, THE Tularosa marshal, brought in Bobby Valdez Thursday afternoon and right away sent a man to Las Cruces to fetch Judge Metairie. Bohannon didn't have a doubt Valdez would not be bound over for trial, and he was right. Friday morning a coroner's jury decided that one Roberto Eladio Viscarra y Valdez did willfully commit murder—judging from the size hole in the forehead of one Harley Tanner (deceased) and the .41-caliber Colt gun found on the accused when he was apprehended the next day. A witness testified that he saw Bobby Valdez pull this same Colt and let go at Tanner in a fashion that in no way resembled self-defense.

Everybody agreed it was about time a smart-aleck gunman like Bobby Valdez was brought to justice and made to pay the penalty. The only ones who'd cry would be some of the girls who couldn't see his handgun for his brown eyes. It was a shame he had to hang, being only twenty-two, but that's what would happen. He didn't have to be bad.

Saturday morning, Criminal Sessions Court, the Honorable Benson Metairie presiding, was called to order in the lobby of the Regent Hotel. The courthouse at Las Cruces would have been better, but that meant transporting Bobby Valdez almost a hundred miles. A year ago he'd gotten away when they were taking him there from Mesilla, and Mesilla was like just across the field.

VALDEZ WAIVED counsel, though there wasn't an attorney in Tularosa to defend him if he'd wanted one. Judge Metairie said it was just as well. Since the case was cut and dried, why waste time with a lot of litigating?

The court called up a witness who swore he'd seen Bobby Valdez plain as day come out of the Regent Café that Wednesday evening, which established the accused's presence in town the night of the shooting.

The star witness took the stand and said he was crossing the street to have a word with his friend Harley Tanner, who was standing right in front of this hotel, when Bobby Valdez came out of the shadows of the adobe building, called Tanner a dirty name, and, when Tanner came around, pulled his gun and shot him. Then Valdez lit out.

Bohannon suggested stepping outside to reenact the crime, but Judge Metairie said everybody knew what the front of the Regent Hotel looked like and the fierce sun this time of day wasn't going to make it any plainer. "Just close your eyes, Ed, and make a picture," the judge told Bohannon.

It was stated that the next morning Bohannon's posse followed Valdez's sign till they caught up with him about noon near the Mescalero reservation line. Valdez's horse had lamed and left Bobby out in the open, as Bohannon said, "with his pants down, so to speak."

Judge Metairie called a man who was referred to as a character witness and this man described seeing Bobby Valdez shoot two men during the White Sands bank holdup last Christmastime. Another character witness was on the Butterfield stage that was held up last June between Lordsburg and Continental. Surer'n hell it was Bobby Valdez who'd opened the door with that .41 Colt gun in his hand, and no polka-dot bandanna over his nose was going to argue it wasn't. Two more men sat down on the Douglas-chair witness stand with like stories.

Judge Metairie looked at his watch and asked what time was the stage back to Las Cruces, and when somebody told him not till three o'clock, he said that they might as well adjourn for dinner then and let the jury reach their verdict over a nice meal—though he didn't see where they'd have much thinking to do.

Court reconvened at one-thirty. The jury foreman stood up, waited for the talking to die, then said how they allowed Bobby Valdez sure couldn't be anything else but guilty.

Judge Metairie nodded, gaveled the register desk to restore order, waited until the quiet could be felt, then in the voice of doom sentenced Roberto Eladio Viscarra y Valdez, on the morning one week from this day, to be hanged by the neck until dead.

Criminal Sessions Court was closed and most people felt Judge Metairie had turned in a better-than-usual performance.

Saturday evening Lyall Quinlan went on duty at the Tularosa Jail.

It came about because Bohannon was scheduled to play poker and Quinlan arrived just at the right time. He came looking for the job; still, he was taken by surprise when Bohannon offered it to him, "temporarily, you understand," because he'd been turned down so many times before. Lyall Quinlan wanted to be a lawman, but Bohannon always put him off with the excuse that he already had an assistant, Barney Groom, and Barney served the purpose even if he was an old man.

But Bohannon was thinking maybe an extra night man ought to be on with Valdez upstairs, a man to sit up there and watch him. He was supposed to play cards tonight, which disallowed him.

Then, lo and behold, there was young Lyall Quinlan coming in the door!

"Lyall, you musta heard me wishin' for you." Then, seeing the astonishment come over the boy's face—a thin face with big, self-conscious eyes—he thought: Hell, Lyall's all right. Even if he doesn't pack much weight, he's honest. And he rode in the posse that brought in Valdez. An eager boy like him'd make a good deputy! For what he considered would be a temporary period, Bohannon convinced himself that Quinlan would do just fine. Tomorrow he could always kick him the hell out. . . .

"Barney, give Lyall here a scattergun and tell him what to do," and Bohannon was gone.

Lyall Quinlan sat up all night watching Bobby Valdez. That is, most of the time he sat in the cane-bottom chair—it was in the hallway facing the one cell they had upstairs—he was keeping his eyes on Valdez, who hardly paid him any attention. Whenever Lyall would start to get sleepy, he'd get up, crook the sawed-off scattergun under his arm, and pace up and down in the short hallway.

The first time he did it, Bobby Valdez, who was lying on his back with his eyes closed, opened them, turned his head enough to see Lyall, and told him to shut up. It was his boots making the noise. But Lyall went right on walking up and down. Valdez called on one of the men saints then and asked him why did all keepers of jails wear squeaky boots? The lamp hanging out in the hall didn't seem to bother him, only Lyall's boots.

When Lyall kept on walking, the Mexican said something else, half smiling—a low-voiced string of soft-spoken Spanish.

Lyall edged closer to the cell and said through the heavy iron bars, "Hush up!"

Valdez went to sleep right after that and Lyall sat in the chair again, feeling pretty good, not so tense anymore.

Let him try something, Lyall thought, watching the sleeping Mexican, feeling the shotgun across his lap. I'd blast him before he got through the door. He practice-swung the gun around. Cut him right in half. Boy, it was heavy. Only about fifteen inches of barrel left and really heavy. Imagine what that'd do to a man!

He kept watching the sleeping man, his eyes going from the high black boots to the lavender shirt and the dark face, the composed, soft-featured dark face.

How can he sleep? Next Saturday he's going to swing from the end of a rope and he's laying there sleeping. Well, some people are built different. If he wasn't different he wouldn't be in that cell. But he ain't more'n a year older than I am. How could he have already done so much in his life? And killed the men he has? Two at White

Sands, one in Mesilla. Tanner. Lyall's thumb went over the tips of his fingers. That's four. Then two more way over to Pima County. At least six, though some claim nine and ten. And Elodie thrilled to death because she served him his dinner the night he shot Tanner. They say he was something with the girls—which about proves that they don't use their heads for much more than a place to grow hair.

Well, he just better not try to come out of that cell. About a minute later Lyall went over and jiggled the door to make sure it was still locked.

Barney Groom came up when it was daylight, and seeing Lyall just sitting there he blinked like he couldn't believe what his eyes told him. "You awake?"

Lyall rose. "Of course."

"Son, you mean you've been awake all night?"

"I thought I was hired to watch this prisoner."

Old Barney Groom shook his head.

"What's the matter?"

"Nothin'," Barney said. Then, "Bohannon's downstairs."

Lyall said, "He want to see me?"

"When you go out he won't be able to help it," said Barney.

"Well, and when should I come back?"

"I ain't the timekeeper. Ask Bohannon about that."

They heard footsteps on the stairs and then Bohannon was in the hallway, yawning, scratching his shirtfront.

Barney Groom said, "Ed, this boy stayed awake all night!"

Bohannon stopped scratching, though he didn't drop his hand. He looked at Lyall Quinlan, who nodded and said, "Mr. Bohannon."

The marshal squinted in the dim light. It was plain he'd been drinking, the way his eyes looked filmy, though he stood there with his feet planted and didn't sway a bit. Finally he said, "You don't say!"

"All night," Barney Groom said.

Bohannon looked at him. "How would you know?"

"He was awake when I come up."

Bohannon said nothing.

"Mr. Bohannon," Lyall said, "I didn't go to sleep."

"Maybe you did and maybe you did not."

Bobby Valdez had been watching them. Now he swung his legs off the bunk. He stood up and moved toward the bars. "He's telling the truth," the Mexican said.

Bohannon put his cold eyes on Valdez for a moment, then looked back at Lyall Quinlan.

Valdez shrugged. "It don't make any difference to me," he said. "But make him grease his boots if he's going to walk all night."

Barney Groom moved a step toward the cell as if threatening Valdez. "You got any more requests?"

"Yes," the Mexican said right away. "I want to go to church."

"What?" Barney Groom said, then was embarrassed for having looked like he'd taken the Mexican seriously, and added, "Sure. I'll send the carriage around."

Valdez looked at him without expression. "This is Sunday."

Bohannon was squinting and half smiling. "Any special denomination, Brother Valdez?"

"Listen, man," Valdez said, "this is Sunday, and I have to go to mass."

Bohannon asked, "You go to mass every Sunday?"

"I've missed some."

Bohannon, with the half smile, went on studying him. Then he said, "Tell you what. We'll douse you with a bucket of holy water instead."

Bohannon and Groom left right after that. Lyall was to stay until one or the other came back from breakfast.

When he was alone again, Lyall looked at Valdez sitting on the bunk. Even after the words were ready he waited a good ten minutes before saying them. "The nearest church is down to White Sands," he told Valdez. "You can't blame the marshal for not wanting to ride you all the way down there."

Valdez looked up.

"It's so far," Lyall Quinlan said. He looked toward the window at the end of the hallway, then back to Valdez. "I appreciate you telling the marshal I was awake all night. I think something like that sets pretty good with him."

Bobby Valdez looked at Lyall curiously. Then his expression softened to a smile, as if he'd suddenly become aware of a new interest, and he said, "Anytime, friend."

When Bohannon came back he sent Lyall across the street to the Regent to get Valdez's breakfast. After he'd given the tray to Valdez, Bohannon deputized him, but mentioned how it was a temporary appointment until the Citizens Committee passed on it. "Now, if you was to keep an extra-special eye on Brother Valdez, I'd have to recommend you as fit, wouldn't I?" He patted Lyall's shoulder and said now was as good a time as any to start the new appointment. "We'll see how you handle yourself alone."

Lyall thought it was a funny way to do things, but he'd have plenty of time for sleep later on. When opportunity knocks on the door you got to open it, he told himself. So he stayed on at the jail, sitting downstairs this time, until midafternoon when Bohannon came back.

"Now get yourself some shut-eye, boy," the marshal told him, "so you'll be in fit shape for tonight."

Lyall's mother told him they were making a fool

out of him, but Lyall didn't have time to argue. He
just said this was what he always wanted to do—a
hell of a lot better than working behind a store
counter, though he didn't use quite those words.
Lyall's mother used mother arguments, but finally
there was nothing she could do but shake her head
and let him go to bed.

HE WENT BACK on duty at nine, sitting in the cane-
bottom chair, not hearing a sound from Barney
Groom downstairs. Bobby Valdez was more talka-
tive. He talked about horses and girls and the terrible fact that he hadn't gotten to church that day;
then made a big to-do admiring Lyall for the way
he could go so long without sleep. That was fine.

But pretty soon Bobby Valdez went to sleep and
that night Lyall walked up and down the little hallway even more than he had the first night. Two or
three times he almost went to sleep, but he kept
moving and blinking his eyes. He found a way of
propping the shotgun between his leg and the chair
arm, so that the trigger guard dug into his thigh and
that kept him awake whenever he sat down to rest.

In the morning Bohannon came up the stairs quietly, but Lyall heard him and said, "Hi, Mr. Bohannon," when the marshal tiptoed in.

Lyall slept all day Monday and after that he was
all right, not having any trouble keeping awake

that night. Bobby Valdez talked to him until late
and that helped.

Tuesday he ate his supper at the Regent Café before going to work. He mentioned weather to
Elodie and how the food was getting better, but
didn't once refer to the silver deputy star on his
shirtfront. Elodie tried to be unconcerned, too, but
finally she just had to ask him, and Lyall answered,
"Why, sure, Elodie, I've been a deputy marshal
since last Saturday. Didn't you know that?"

Elodie had to describe how Bobby Valdez came
in for dinner the night he shot Tanner. "He sat right
on that very stool you're on and ate tacos like he
didn't have a worry in the world. Real calm."

Lyall said, "Uh-huh, but he's kind of a little
squirt, ain't he?" and walked out casually, knowing
Elodie was watching after him with her mouth open.

TUESDAY NIGHT Valdez told Lyall how his being in
the cell had all come about—how he'd started out
an honest vaquero down in Sonora, but got mixed
up with some unprincipled men who were chousing
other people's cows. Bobby Valdez said, by the
name of a saint, he didn't know anything about it,
but the next thing the *rurales* were chasing him
across the border. About a year later, in Contention, Arizona, he killed a man. It was in self-
defense and he was acquitted; but the man had a

friend, so he ended up killing the friend too. And after that it was just one thing leading to another. Everybody seemed to take him wrong . . . couldn't get an honest job . . . so what was a young man supposed to do?

The way he described it made Lyall Quinlan shake his head and say it was a shame.

Wednesday night Bobby Valdez only nodded to Lyall when he came on duty. The Mexican was sitting on the edge of the bunk, elbows on his knees, staring at his hands as he washed them together absently.

He's finally realizing he's going to die, Lyall thought. You have to leave a man alone when he's doing that. So for over an hour no one spoke.

When Lyall did speak it was because he wanted to make it a little easier for Valdez. He said, "All people have to die. That's the best way to look at it."

Valdez looked up, then nodded thoughtfully.

"You got to look at it," Lyall went on, "like, well, just something that happens to everybody."

"I've done that," the Mexican said. "What torments me now is that I have not confessed."

"You didn't have to," Lyall said. "Judge Metairie found out the facts without you confessing."

"No, I mean to a priest."

"Oh."

"It is a terrible thing to die without absolution."

"Oh."

It was quiet then, Lyall frowning, the Mexican

looking at his hands. But suddenly Bobby Valdez looked up, his face brightening, and he said, as if it had just occurred to him, "My friend, would *you* bring a priest to me?"

"Well—I'll tell Mr. Bohannon in the morning. I'm sure he'll—"

"No!" Valdez stood up quickly. "I cannot take the chance of letting him know!" His voice calmed as he said, "You know how he makes fun of things spiritual—that about the holy water, and calling me 'Brother.' What if he should refuse this request? Then I would die in the state of mortal sin just because he does not understand. My friend," he said just above a whisper, "surely you can see that he must not know."

"Well—" Lyall said.

"In White Sands," Valdez said quickly, "there is a man called Sixto Henriquez who knows the priest well. At the mescal shop they'll tell you where he lives. Now, all you would have to do is tell Sixto to send the priest late Friday night after it is very quiet, and then it will be accomplished."

Lyall hesitated.

"Then," Valdez said solemnly, "I would not die in sin."

Lyall thought about it some more and finally he nodded.

He woke up at noon for the ride to White Sands. He'd have to hurry to be back in time to go on duty; but he would have hurried anyway because he didn't feel right about what he was doing, as if it was something sneaky. At the mescal shop the proprietor directed him, in as few words as were necessary, to the adobe of Sixto Henriquez. Lyall was half afraid and half hoping Sixto wouldn't be home. But there he was, a thin little man in a striped shirt who didn't open the door all the way until Lyall mentioned Valdez.

After Lyall had told why he was there, Henriquez took his time rolling a cigarette. He lit it and blew out smoke and then said, "All right."

Lyall rode back to Tularosa feeling a lot better. That hadn't been hard at all.

When he went on duty that night he said to Bobby Valdez, "You're all set," and would just as soon have let it go at that, but Valdez insisted that he tell him everything. He told him. There wasn't much to it—how the man just said, "All right." But Valdez seemed to be satisfied.

Friday morning Lyall stopped at the Regent Café for his breakfast. Elodie was serving the counter. She was frowning and muttering about being switched to mornings just the day before Bobby Valdez's hanging.

Lyall told her, "A nice girl like you don't want to see a hanging."

"It's the principle of it," she pouted. The principle being everybody in Tularosa was excited about

Bobby Valdez hanging whether they had a stomach for it or not.

"Lyall, don't you get scared up there alone with him?" she said with a little shiver that might have been partly real.

"What's there to be scared of? He's locked in a cell."

"What if one of his friends should come to help him?" Elodie said.

"How could a man like that have friends?"

"Well—I worry about you, Lyall."

Lyall stopped being calm, his whole face grinning. "Do you, Elodie?"

And that's what Lyall was thinking about when he went on duty Friday night. About Elodie.

Barney Groom was sitting at Bohannon's rolltop with his feet propped up, looking like he was ready to go to sleep. He said to Lyall, " 'Night's the last night. After the hanging we can relax a little."

Lyall went upstairs and sat down in the cane-bottom chair still thinking about Elodie: how she looked like a little girl when she pouted. A deputy marshal can probably support a wife, he thought. Still, he wasn't so sure, since Bohannon hadn't mentioned salary to him yet.

Bobby Valdez said, "This is the night the priest comes."

Lyall looked up. "I almost forgot. Bet you feel better already."

"As if I have risen from the dead," Bobby Valdez said.

Later on—Lyall didn't have a timepiece on him but he estimated it was shortly after midnight—he heard the noise downstairs. Not a strange noise; it was just that it came unexpectedly in the quiet. He looked over at Bobby Valdez. Still asleep. For the next few minutes it was quiet again.

Then he heard footsteps on the stairs. It must be the priest, Lyall thought, getting up. He'd told the man to tell the priest to just walk by Barney, who'd probably be asleep, and if he wasn't, just explain the whole thing. So Barney was either asleep or had agreed.

Lyall wasn't prepared for the robed figure that stepped into the hallway. He'd expected a priest in a regular black suit; but then he remembered the priest at White Sands was the kind who wore a long robe and sandals.

Lyall said, "Father?"

That end of the hallway was darker and Lyall couldn't see him very well, and now as he came forward, Lyall still couldn't see his face because the cowl, the hood part of the robe, was up over his head. His arms were folded, with his hands up in the big sleeves.

"Father?"

"My son."

Lyall turned to the cell. "He's right here, Father."

Valdez was standing at the bars and it struck Lyall suddenly that he hadn't heard Valdez get up. He turned his head to look at the priest and felt the gun barrel jab against his back.

"Place your weapon on the floor," the voice behind him said.

Bobby Valdez added, "My son," smiling now.

THE MAN BEHIND Lyall reached past him to hand the ring of jail keys to Valdez. As he did, the cowl fell back and Lyall saw the man he'd talked to in White Sands. Sixto Henriquez.

Valdez said, "Whether you could get a robe was the thing that bothered me."

"A gift," Sixto said. "Hanging from his clothesline."

Lyall heard them, but he wouldn't let himself believe it. He wanted to say, "Wait a minute! Come on, now, this wasn't supposed to happen!"

Thinking of Bohannon and Elodie and the nights walking in the hallway, suddenly knowing he'd done the wrong thing, and too late to do anything about it. "Wait a minute . . . I was trying to help you!" But not saying it because it had been his own damn, stupid fault, and he was so aware of it now, he had to bite his lip to keep from yelling like a kid.

Valdez came out of the cell and picked up the shotgun Lyall had dropped. He said to Lyall, "Now my soul feels better."

He motioned Sixto toward the stairs. "Go first and see how it is with the old one."

"He sleep," Sixto said, and patted the barrel of his pistol.

"Let's be sure," Bobby Valdez said. He watched Sixto go through the doorway and listened to him start down the stairs. He looked at Lyall again, smiling. "You can mark this to experience."

If Valdez had backed out, holding the gun on Lyall, it wouldn't have happened. Even if he had just warned Lyall not to yell out or follow them—but he just turned and started walking out, *knowing* Lyall wouldn't dare try to stop him. And that's where Bobby Valdez made his mistake.

Lyall saw the man's back like a slap in the face. Even though he was scared, all of a sudden the knots inside him got too tight to stand. No thinking now about how it happened or what might happen—just an overpowering urge to get him!

He lunged at the back that was moving away. Three long strides and his arms were around Valdez's neck, jerking, swinging him off his feet. He heard the shotgun clatter against the wall and hit the floor.

Tight against him, Bobby Valdez was turning his

body. Lyall let go with one arm, brought it down quick, and drove it as hard as he could into the stomach almost against him. Valdez gasped and started to sag. Then footsteps on the stairs. Lyall scrambled for the shotgun, came up with it, and was at the doorway in time to see Sixto partway up the stairs, but as he raised the shotgun there was a swirl of robes and Sixto was at the bottom again. There was the sound of him running through the office, then nothing. Lyall came around fast. Valdez was almost on him, coming in low, diving for Lyall's legs—and he dove right into the shotgun barrel swung hard against his skull.

Lyall just stood there breathing for a minute before he dragged Bobby Valdez back to the cell and hefted him onto the bunk.

"Mr. Valdez," Lyall said out loud, "that's one *you* can mark to experience."

He went downstairs after that. Barney Groom was slouched in his chair, out cold. Lyall went to the doorway; he stepped outside to have a look around, and there was the friar's robe. It was in the road over by the hitch rack. Lyall gathered it up quick. He brought it back in the office and hung it beneath his rain slicker that was hooked on a peg. Then he breathed easier.

★　★　★

ELODIE TURNED AWAY from the window. "It's over, Lyall," she said gravely. "They're starting to come out on the street."

Lyall glanced at her. "Is that right, Elodie?" he said, then put a little more ketchup on his eggs. Scrambled eggs were good that way; this morning they tasted even better. He ate them, half smiling, remembering Bohannon coming that morning. Bohannon frowning at Barney Groom, Barney trying to figure how he got his head bumped when he was sound asleep.

Then when they went upstairs—that was really something. Bohannon saying, "Maybe he's sick," seeing Valdez's white face and the side of his head swollen like a lopsided melon. And Barney Groom saying, "Maybe the same bug bit me, bit him."

Then what Bohannon said to him when they went downstairs again—that was the best.

"Now, Lyall, you done a fair job, though just sitting up there trying to keep awake wasn't much of a test. Tell you what"—Bohannon pulled a folded sheet of paper from his vest pocket—"last night I got a note from the White Sands marshal telling about the padre there getting his outfit stolen off the clothesline and would I assign a man to it since he's busy collecting taxes." Bohannon chuckled. "Have to keep the padres happy. Now, Lyall, if you

could prove to me you're smart enough to get that
padre's robe back for him, I'll see you're made a
permanent deputy. And that's my solemn word."

Lyall pretended he didn't see Bohannon wink at
Barney Groom. He said, "Yes, sir, I'll sure try." Just
as serious as he could.

Man with the Iron Arm

★

Chapter One

CHRIS AND KITE and Vicente were already half down the slope when we came out of the trees— three riders spread out and running hard, waving their sombreros like they could smell the mescal we'd been talking about all morning. This new man, Tobin Royal, was next to me holding in his big sorrel I think just to show he could hold himself, too, if he wanted. He was smoking a cigarette and squinting through the smoke curling up from it.

At the bottom of the grade, looking bleached white in the big open sunlight, were the adobes of

Brady's Store: one main structure and a few scattered out-buildings and a corral. Brady's served as a Hatch & Hodges stage-line stop, besides being a combination store and saloon for the half dozen one-loop ranchers in the vicinity. The one we worked for—the El Centro Cattle Company—was bigger than all of them put together twice and just the eastern tip of it came close to touching Brady's Store. Chris and Kite and Vicente and this Tobin Royal and I were gathering stock from the east range, readying for a trail drive and we felt we deserved some of Brady's mescal long as it was handy.

By the time Tobin and I rode into the yard, the others had gone into the saloon side of the adobe and I saw a bare-headed, dark-haired man leading their three horses over to the open stable shed that attached to the adobe. He looked around, hearing us ride in, and I saw then that he had only one arm. For a moment he stood looking at us; then he turned, leading the horses away, moving slow like he either had all the time in the world or else his mind was on something else.

As we swung off, this Tobin Royal called over to him, "Hey, boy, two more here!" But the one-armed man kept going like he hadn't heard. Tobin stood looking at the rumps of the three horses moving into the stable. He let his reins drop and he moved a half dozen slow strides toward the stable. A quirt was thonged to his left wrist and it hung limp at his side opposite the long-barreled Navy Colt on his right hip.

He was a slim, good-looking boy, but he never smiled unless he said something he thought was funny, and he liked to pose, as he was doing now with the quirt and his hat tilted forward and the low-slung Navy Colt. In the few weeks he'd been with us I'd learned this about him.

I started to bring the horses and he turned his head. "You keep them horses over there."

"What's the difference? I'll take them over."

"Just stay where you are." His gaze went back to the stable as the one-armed fellow came out of the shadow into the sunlight again, and for a moment Tobin just stared at the man.

"Are you deaf or something?"

☆ ☆ ☆

THE MAN TURNED to Tobin and his eyes looked tired. They were watery, and with the bits of straw sticking to his shirt and pants he looked as if he'd just slept off a drunk in the stable. He was about thirty, a year one way or the other. He didn't answer Tobin, but came on toward me.

"I asked you a question!"

He stopped then and looked at Tobin.

"I asked you," Tobin said, "if you were deaf."

"No, I'm not deaf."

"You work here?"

The man nodded.

"You're supposed to answer when somebody calls."

"I'll try to remember that," the man said.

The temper rose in Tobin's face again. "Listen, don't talk like that to me! I'll kick your hind end across the yard!"

The tired eyes looked at me momentarily. He came on then and took the reins and started back toward the stable with the horses. Tobin called to him, "Water and rub 'em down now . . . you hear me?" He stood looking after the horses for a time, then finally he turned and started for the adobe as I did.

"You didn't have to talk to him like that."

Tobin shook his head disgustedly. "Judas, I hate a slow-moving, worthless man."

"He had only one arm," I said.

"What difference does that make?"

"Maybe it makes him feel bad."

"It don't make him walk slower."

"Well maybe some men it does."

Tobin opened the door and walked in ahead of me over to the bar that was along the left-hand wall where Chris and Kite and Vicente stood leaning and drinking mescal, and he said, "Whiskey," to Brady standing behind the bar.

Brady was looking toward me, waiting for Tobin

to get out of the way. "How you been, Uncle?" Brady said to me.

"Fair," I told him. "How've you been?"

"Good." He smiled now, that big, loose-faced, double-chinned smile of his. "It's nice to see you again."

"I want whiskey," Tobin said.

Brady looked at him. "I heard you, Sonny. You can't wait till I tell a friend hello?"

I got to the bar before Tobin could say anything. "Joe, this is Tobin Royal, a new man with us."

Tobin nodded and Joe Brady said glad-to-meet-you, because he was a businessman. He sat the whiskey bottle on the bar and poured a drink out of it. Tobin emptied the hooker, and touched the bottle with the glass for another. But this one, after Brady poured it, he took to one of the three tables that were along the other wall, where the stage passengers ate. He sat down with the drink in front of him and started making a cigarette.

Joe Brady nudged the mescal bottle toward me. "What's he trying to prove?"

"That he's older than he is," I answered. I could hear Vicente telling a vaquero story and Chris and Kite were listening, knowing what the ending was, but waiting for it anyway. They didn't have much to say to Tobin, because the first day he joined us he had a fight with Kite.

Kite had been a Tascosa buffalo skinner, a big rawboned boy, but Tobin licked him good. Tobin always stayed a few steps out from them, like he didn't want to be mistaken for just an ordinary rider.

"I see you got a new man too," I said to Brady.

"That's John Lefton," Brady said. "He came here on the stage a few weeks ago . . . got off like he expected to see something. As it turned out, he'd paid the fare as far as his money would take him . . . which was to here."

"What's he running away from?"

"Did you see him close?"

"You mean the one arm?"

Brady nodded. "That's what I *think* he's running from."

"Well, it's too bad. How'd he lose it?"

"In the War."

"Well," I said again, "it's better to lose it that way than, say, in a corncrusher. What side was he on?"

"Union."

"Don't hold it against him, Joe."

"Hell, the War's been over for eight years."

"You felt sorry for him and gave him a job?"

Brady shrugged. "What else could I do?"

"He looks like he drinks."

"He about draws his wages in mescal. But he

does his work . . . better'n the Mex boy and even took over the bookkeeping."

"It's a terrible thing to see a man down like that."

I heard the screen door open behind me and Brady mumbled, "Here he is."

Chapter Two

I half turned as he went by, walking to the back part of the adobe where Brady's rolltop desk was next to the door that led to the store part. He was carrying a push-broom.

Brady called over the bar, "John, you don't have to do that now."

"It's all right," he answered. His voice sounded natural, but like there wasn't a speck of enthusiasm in him if he ever wanted to bring it out.

"No," Brady said. "Wait till later. These people will just mess up the place anyhow."

He nodded, then leaned the push-broom against the wall and stood at the desk with his back to us.

"I never know how to talk to him," Brady half whispered.

"Mr. Brady—"

Brady looked up and saw John Lefton at the end

of the bar now. As he walked down to him, Chris and Kite and Vicente stopped talking. They stood at the bar pretending like they weren't trying to hear what was said, as Brady and the one-armed man talked for a minute. Then Brady came back for the mescal bottle and poured him a good shot of it.

"I wonder what he's trying to forget," I said, when Brady was opposite me again.

"His wife," Brady said, and didn't add anything to that for a minute. Then he said, "He's been here three weeks and he's gotten three letters from her, forwarded from the last town he stayed in, but he hasn't answered one."

"How do you know it's his wife . . . he told you?"

Brady hesitated. "I read one of the letters."

"Joe!"

He gritted his teeth, meaning for me to keep my voice down. "After he got the last one he started drinking and kept it up till it put him asleep. He was sitting at that table there and the letter was right in front of him. Listen . . . I just stood there trying to figure him out, wanting to help him, but I couldn't help him till I knew what his trouble was. Finally I decided, hell, there's only one way to do it, read the letter."

"Go on."

"She asked him why he never answered any of her letters and when he was going to send for her, and telling how much she loved him," Brady paused. "You see it now?"

I COULD SEE IT all right. Him coming back from the War lacking an arm and somehow figuring he'd be a burden and being sensitive about how he looked. Then running away to prove himself . . . then doing more running than proving. Promising to send for her at first, but each day knowing it would be harder as the time passed. Her at home waiting while he wanders around losing his self-respect. That would be eight years of waiting now.

"Maybe," I said, "he don't want her anymore."

Brady shook his head. "You never saw him read the letters."

About a minute later, this Tobin Royal came up next to me and slapped his left-handed quirt down on the bar. "Give me another one," he said.

Brady said civilly, "You haven't paid for the first two yet."

"We'll settle when I'm through," Tobin told him. He drank off part of the whiskey that Brady poured and stood fiddling with what was left, turning the glass between two fingers. His eyes lifted as Brady moved down the bar to where John Lefton was standing and poured him another mescal.

Tobin leaned away from the bar to look at

Lefton. He came back then and said, loud enough for everybody to hear, "I guess even a man without all his parts can drink mescal."

I couldn't believe he'd said it, but there it was and at that moment the room was quiet as night. I half whispered to Tobin, "What'd you say that for?" But he didn't answer me. He moved from the bar the next moment and went down to stand next to Lefton who glanced at him, but looked down at his drink again.

"Before you go sloppin' up the mescal juice," Tobin said, "I want to understand my horse is cared for. You rubbed him good?"

Lefton was raising the mescal glass, ignoring Tobin, and suddenly Tobin's quirt came up and lashed down on Lefton's arm and the mescal glass went slamming skidding over the bar.

"I asked you a question," Tobin said.

For a shaded second Lefton's face came alive, but as fast as it came the anger faded from his eyes and he looked down at his wrist, holding it tightly to his stomach. "No," he answered then. "I didn't rub down your horse."

"Do it now," Tobin said.

Brady moved toward them. "Wait a minute! You don't order my help around!"

"He wants to do it," Tobin answered. "Don't you?"

Lefton's eyes raised. "It's all right, Mr. Brady."

"I'll tip him something," Tobin grinned. He looked at Lefton again. "One hand's as good as two for rubbing down a horse, ain't it?"

Lefton hesitated. Before he could answer Tobin's quirt came down cracking against the bar edge and Lefton went back half a step.

"You're not much for answering questions, are you?"

Lefton's eyes raised momentarily. "I'll tend to your horse."

Tobin grinned. "I want to ask you something else." He waited to make Lefton speak.

"All right," Lefton said.

"Where did you leave your arm?"

Again Lefton hesitated and you had the urge to poke him to make him hurry up and answer. "On Rock Creek," he said then. "East of Cemetery Ridge."

"What was your outfit?"

"Seventh Michigan."

Tobin's face brightened. "Damn, I thought you looked like a blue-belly! One of Wade Hampton's boys cut you good, didn't he?" He looked around at the rest of us and said, "A brother of mine was with Wade, all the way to Yellow Tavern."

Lefton didn't say a word and Tobin studied him. "What rank did you hold?"

"Lieutenant."

"From lieutenant of cavalry to rubbin' down

horses," Tobin said. He stuck out his quirt as Lefton started to walk past him. "I didn't say you could go!" The quirt moved across Lefton's chest and the tip of it poked at the empty right sleeve.

"Above the elbow," Tobin said. "Were you right-handed or left?"

"Right."

"Now that'd be a hardship," Tobin said. "Teaching the left what the right used to know." The quirt end kept slapping gently at the empty sleeve as he spoke. "But the left's good enough for sloppin' mescal juice, huh?"

Lefton did not answer.

"You hear me?"

"Yes . . . it's good enough."

"I thought stable boys were supposed to say yes *sir*."

"That's enough!" Brady said. His big face was red and had a tight look about the mouth. "You leave him alone now!"

Tobin looked at Brady. "You ought to learn your stable boy proper respect."

"This man isn't a stable boy!"

"Then how come he wants to rub down my horse?"

This was carrying it too far. I knew Tobin could lick me eight ways from breakfast with one hand, but now I could feel the anger up in my throat and I had to say something.

"Tobin . . . you stop that kind of talk and act like a human being for once in your life!"

He took the time to look my way. "Uncle, are you telling me what to do?"

"I can't talk any plainer!"

He grinned . . . didn't get mad . . . just grinned and said, "Uncle, you know better than that. You don't tell me what to do. Not you or any man here." He turned to Lefton again. "I'm the only one doing any telling, ain't that right?"

He poked Lefton with the quirt and Lefton nodded, though he was looking at the floor.

"Let me hear you say it."

Lefton nodded again. "Yes . . . that's right."

Tobin waited. "Yes . . . what?"

Then it was like seeing this Lefton give up the last shred of pride he owned, and you had to turn your head because you knew he was going to say it, and you didn't want to be looking at him because you weren't sure if you'd feel sorry for him anymore.

We heard it all right, the hollow sounding, "*Yes sir—*"

And after it, Tobin saying, "Now you find your left-handed curry-comb and go on out and rub my horse."

★

Chapter Three

All the way back to our headquarters, later on, with the two-hundred-odd head we'd gathered, not one of us said a word to Tobin, though he made some remarks when we stopped that night as to how fine his big sorrel looked even if it had been curried by a left-handed stable boy.

As I said, we'd come over to the east range to gather and by the time we'd got back to the home ranch the trail drive was about to get under way and, thank the Lord, we saw little of Tobin for the next forty-some-odd days. Chris and Kite and Vicente and I were swing riders when we were on the move; but Tobin, because he was a new man, had to ride drag and eat dust all the way.

We left Sudan, where the El Centro main herd was headquartered, about the first of May, and it wasn't till the middle of June that I had my bath in the Grand Central Hotel in Ellsworth.

I'll tell you the truth: I thought of that one-armed man about every day of the drive, though I never talked about him to the others.

Still, I knew they were thinking about him the way I was. Picturing him standing there with his one arm held tight against his belly after Tobin had

quirted him—holding it like that because he didn't
have another hand to rub the sting with. Maybe we
should all have jumped Tobin and beat his hide off,
but that wouldn't have proved anything. I think we
were all waiting to see this one-armed man stand his
ground and fight back, and though he wouldn't have
had a chance, at least he would have felt better after.

Why did Tobin lay it on him? I don't know. I've
seen men like Tobin before and since, but not many,
thank the Lord. That kind always has to be proving
something that other people don't even bother about.
Maybe Tobin did it to show us he had no use for a
man who couldn't stand on his own two feet. Maybe
he did it just so he could see how low a man could
slip. Then he could say to himself, "Tobin, boy, you'll
never be like that, even if both your arms were gone."

And probably Tobin would be judging himself
right. No one could say that he wasn't like a piece of
rawhide. He was hard on himself even, would take
the meanest horse in the remuda and be the last one
in at night just so he could say he worked harder than
anybody else. But that's all you could say for him.

And why did John Lefton, a man who had been a
cavalry officer and gone through the war, stand
there and take it? That I don't know either. Maybe
he had *too much* pride.

After running for eight years, it was a long way
to look back to what he was. And the mescal would
blur it to make it farther. I remember sitting in the

tub in the Grand Central Hotel and saying, "The hell with him," like that was final. But it wasn't that easy. There was something about him that told you that at least one time he had been much man.

We did see John Lefton again.

No . . . I don't want to jump to it. I'll tell it the way it happened.

We came back from Ellsworth and most of that fall Chris and me worked a company herd up on the Canadian near Tascosa. Then toward the middle of November we were ordered back to Sudan. One day, right after we were back, the company man, C. H. Felt, said he was sending us over to the east range with a wagon full of alfalfa to scatter for the winter graze. I asked him who was going and he said Chris and Kite and Vicente . . . that's right, and Tobin Royal.

★ ★ ★

THAT'S HOW THE same five of us come to ride down that gray windy grade into Brady's yard that November afternoon.

No one was in sight, not even the dog we could hear barking off somewhere behind the adobes. Kite swung down and took my reins as I dismounted. Vicente took Chris's. That left Tobin Royal to care for his own. He was still riding that big sorrel.

Chris and I went inside the adobe and right away Chris said, "Something's different here."

"You just never seen the place empty, is all."

He kept looking all around to see if he could place what it was. Then I started looking around and it was an unnaturally long moment before it dawned on me what it was.

The place was *clean*. Not just swept clean and dusted, but there was wax on the bar and three tables and fresh paint on the places it belonged.

"Chris, the place is *clean*. That's what it is!"

He didn't answer me. Chris was looking down to the back end where the rolltop and the door was. A woman, a black-haired, slim-built, prettier-than-ordinary woman, closed the door and came toward us.

She came right up and gave us a little welcome smile, and said, "May I serve you gentlemen something to eat?" Her voice was pleasant, but she seemed to be holding back a little.

Chris said, "Eat?"

And I said, "We ate at camp, ma'am," touching my hat. "We were thinking of a drink."

She smiled again and you could tell that one was put on. "The bar is Mr. Brady's department," she said and started to turn. "He can't be far. I'll see if I can find him." She started to walk to the back, and that's when Kite and Vicente and Tobin Royal came in.

She looked around, but must have reasoned they were with Chris and me, because she went on then until Tobin called out, "Hey . . . where you going?"

She stopped, turning full around as Tobin

brushed past us saying, "Now that old man's using his head," meaning Brady, I guess.

The smile didn't show this time, but she said, "May I serve you something to eat?"

Tobin grinned. "Not to eat."

"I don't serve the bar," the woman said. "Mr. Brady does that."

"Uh-huh," Tobin said. Then he laughed out loud. "Like you never been behind a bar before! What're you doing here then?"

"I'm here," she said quietly, "with my husband."

"You're married to *Brady*?"

"I'm Mrs. Lefton."

"Lefton!" Tobin's mouth hung open. "You're married to that one-armed stable boy!"

The color came up over her face like she'd been slapped, but she didn't say a word. Tobin was grinning and shaking his head like it was the funniest thing he'd ever heard of. "Listen," he said to her. "You get me a whiskey drink and I'll tell you something about your husband you probably don't know."

Right then Brady came in behind us. His coat was on and he was breathing in and out like he'd hurried. From the look on his face you could tell he'd seen our horses and the El Centro brand and the chances were good he knew who he'd find.

The woman said quickly, "Is my husband coming?" and now sounded frightened and as if she were trying hard to keep from crying.

Tobin added, "Or is he busy cleaning the stable?"

"He's breaking a horse," Brady stated.

I said, "Breaking a *horse*?"

Brady turned on me. "That's what I said, breaking a horse!"

Tobin must have been as surprised as any of us; but he wouldn't show it. He just shrugged. "Well, I guess one wing's as good as two for that anyway." Without her expecting it he grabbed Mrs. Lefton's arm. "Honey, your husband waits on me. Why shouldn't you?" He gave her a little push toward the bar and that snaky quirt of his slapped backhanded across where her bustle was.

Brady said something, but I don't know what . . . because I heard a step behind me. I just glanced, then came full around realizing who it was. John Lefton.

Chapter Four

But not the John Lefton we had seen the last time. He didn't have on a hat and his wool shirt was dirty from sweat and dust. His hair was cut shorter than before and hung down a little over his forehead; his jaw was clean-shaved, but he was wearing a full-grown cavalry kind of mustache. That's where the big difference was: the mustache, and the eyes that were dark and clear and looking straight ahead to Tobin.

He walked past us and as he did I saw the quirt hanging from his wrist. I remembered Brady saying that he'd been breaking a horse, but somehow you got the idea he was wearing it for another reason.

He walked right up to Tobin and said, without wasting breath, "Mr. Royal, I've been waiting some months to see you again."

Tobin was half smiling, but you could tell it was put on, while he tried to figure out the change in this man. Tobin moved a little bit. He cocked his hip and leaned his hand on the bar to show he was relaxed.

"First," John Lefton said, "I want to thank you for what you did."

Tobin frowned then. "What'd I do?"

"If you don't know," Lefton said, "I'm not going to explain it. But you must know what I'm going to give you."

Tobin still looked puzzled. He didn't say anything and suddenly Lefton's quirt slashed across Tobin's hand on the edge of the bar.

"You know now?"

Tobin knew. Maybe he couldn't believe it, but he knew and in the instant he was pushing himself from the bar, dipping that stung hand to get at the Navy Colt. The barrel was just clear of the holster when Lefton's quirt cracked Tobin's wrist like a pistol shot, and slapped the Colt right out of his hand. For a moment Tobin was wide open, not sure what to do. Then he saw it coming and tried to cover, but not soon enough and Lefton's quirt lashed across his face cutting him from cheekbone to nose. The quirt came back, catching him across the forehead and his hat went spinning.

Tobin threw up his arms to cover his face, but now Lefton let go of the quirt. He came up with a fist under Tobin's jaw, and when Tobin's guard came apart, the same fist chopped back-handed, like a counterpunch, and smacked hard. This man knew how to fight. The fist swung low again, into Tobin's belly, and when he doubled up, Lefton's knee came up against his jaw. That straightened Tobin good. When he was just about upright the fist came around like a sledgehammer and the next second Tobin was spread-eagle on the floor.

He must have been conscious, though I don't know how; for then Lefton looked down at him and said, "You know what you're going to do now, don't you? As soon as you find a left-handed currycomb."

We just stood there until he got Tobin to his feet and out the door; then Brady said, "Mrs. Lefton, you've got yourself a man." And the way he said *man*, it meant everything it could mean plus how Joe Brady felt about the matter.

Mrs. Lefton smiled. "I've known that for some time," she said mildly—to tell us that there had never been any doubt about it as far as she was concerned. She excused herself right after that.

As soon as the door closed behind her, Brady, like a little kid with a story to tell, filled in the part we didn't know about.

He said on that day last May, after we'd gone, Lefton came back in and poured himself a mescal drink. But he didn't drink it. He just stared at it for the longest time. Maybe fifteen or twenty minutes. Suddenly, then, he swept the drink off and brought his fist down on the bar hard enough to break a bone. He held on to the bar then with his head down and Brady said he thought the man was going to cry. But he never did, and after a minute he went outside.

★ ★ ★

THE CHANGE IN him began right after that, Brady told. It was as if Tobin's quirt had jolted him back to reality. He found himself at deep bottom and now there was only one direction to go, if he had the guts.

Not until a few days later, Brady said, did he realize that Lefton had stopped drinking. He started drawing his wages, did his work all right, and about the middle of July he disappeared for three days. When he came back he had four mustangs on a string. The next day he built a mesquite corral off back of the adobes and that night he wrote a letter to his wife.

By the time his wife arrived, the end of August,

Lefton had broken and sold better than a dozen horses. Understand now, when he started this he didn't know the first thing about breaking horses. What happened was, the time he disappeared, he went to Sudan to find something to invest in with the money he'd saved. He happened to talk to a mustanger who told him there was money in horse trading if he could stand getting his insides jolted up.

Lefton hired a couple of Tonkawa boys to scare up green horses and from that day on he was in business. The mustanger in Sudan taught him a few things, but most of it Lefton learned himself. The hard way. He took a beating from those horses, but he never quit and Brady said it was like watching a man do penance. Maybe Lefton felt the same way about it, I don't know.

Brady said that two weeks ago, when Lefton's count had reached forty sold he'd wondered why Lefton stayed around instead of expanding and locating where business would be better. Brady said today, though, he understood why Lefton had *wanted* to stay.

We all agreed that what we saw that afternoon was one of the finest experiences of our lives. Still, neither Chris, Kite, Vicente or me ever talked about it to anyone. You couldn't tell the second part without telling the first, and we still didn't want to do that.

Tobin Royal stayed with us. I'll give him credit

for that. Working with us after what we'd seen. After that day he didn't talk so much. But those times he did start, after a few drinks or something, I'd look at him and touch my cheek. His fingers would go up and feel where the quirt had lashed him and he would shut up. There was no scar there, but maybe there was to Tobin. One that would always stay with him.

The Longest Day of His Life

Chapter One

New Job

THROUGH THE down-pointed field glasses, his gaze inched from left to right along the road that twisted narrowly through the ravine. Where he sat, hunched forward with his legs crossed and with his elbows resting on raised knees to steady the field glasses, the ground dropped away before him in a long grassy sweep; though across from him the slope climbed steeply into dwarf oak and above the trees a pale-orange wall of sandstone rose seamed and shadowed into sun glare. Below and to the right, the road passed into tree shadow and seemed to end there.

"How far to Glennan's place?"

"About four miles," the man who was next to him kneeling on one knee said. He was twice the age of the man with the field glasses, nearing fifty, and studying the end of the ravine his eyes half closed, tightening his face in a teeth-clenched grimace. His name was Joe Mauren, in charge of road construction for the Hatch & Hodges Stage Line Company.

"Past the trees," Mauren said, "the road drops down through a draw for maybe two miles. You come to grass then and you think you're out of it, but follow the wagon tracks and you go down through another pass. Then you're out and you'll see the house back off a ways. It's built close to deep pinyon and sometimes you can't see it for shadows, but you will this time of day."

"Then twelve miles beyond it to the Rock of Ages mine," Steve Brady, the man with the field glasses, said.

"About that," Mauren said.

The field glasses moved left again. "Will you have to do any work along here?"

"No, those scrub oaks catch anything that falls."

"Just back where you're working now."

"That's the only dangerous place."

"The mine's been hauling through for three months," Brady said. "Rock slides don't worry them."

"The driver of an eight-team ore wagon isn't a stage full of passengers," Mauren said. "If we expect people to ride over this stretch, we have to make it near presentable."

"So two miles back to your construction site and eight back of that to Contention," Steve Brady said. He lowered the field glasses. "Twenty-six miles from Contention to Rock of Ages."

"You'll go far," Mauren said dryly.

"I see why we need a stop at Glennan's place," Brady said.

Mauren nodded. "To calm their nerves and slack their thirst."

"Will Glennan serve whiskey?"

"He blame well better," Mauren said, rising. "Else you don't give him the franchise. That's an unwritten rule, boy." He watched Brady get to his feet, brushing his right leg and the seat of his pants.

"New job, new suit," Mauren said. "And by the time you get to Glennan's the suit's going to be powder-colored instead of dark gray."

Brady turned, his free hand brushing the lapels now. "Does it look all right?"

"About a size too small. You look all hands,
Steve. Like you're ready to grab something."
Mauren almost smiled. "Like that little Kitty
Glennan."

"She must be something, the way you talk."

"It'll make the tears run out of your eyes, Steve.
She's that pretty."

"The suit's all right then, huh?"

"Take the shooter off and you'll be able to button it." Mauren was looking at the Colt that Brady
wore on his right hip.

"It feels good open," Brady said.

Mauren studied him up and down. "Suits are
fine, but you get used to wearing them and before
you know it you're up in Prescott behind a desk.
Like your pa."

"That might'n be so bad."

"You try it, boy. A week and you'd go back to driving or shotgun riding just to get away." They mounted
their horses and Mauren said, "You've wasted enough
time. Now do something for your pay."

"I'll try and come back this way," Brady said.

"Do that now," Mauren answered. He reined
tightly and moved off through the pinyon pine.

* * *

FOR A MOMENT Brady watched him, then slipped
the glasses into a saddlebag, tight-turned his own
mount and slanted down the slope to the road be-

low. He reached the end of the ravine and followed the double wagon ruts into the trees, feeling the relief of the shade now and he pushed his hat up from his forehead, thinking then: Maybe I should've got a new one. The tan Stetson was dusty and dark-stained around the band, but it felt good.

The fact was, everything felt good. It was good to be here and good to see the things there were to see and good to be going where he was going.

He thought of Mr. Glennan whom he had never seen before—Mr. J. F. Glennan—and tried to picture him.

"Mr. Glennan, my name's Brady, with Hatch and Hodges, come with the franchise agreement for you to sign." No—

"Hello Mr. Glennan, my name's Brady, with Hatch and Hodges—you sure got a nice place. Fine for a stage stop, trees for shade and not much building on to do. Here's the agreement, Mr. Glennan. I think you'll like working for"—no—"being with the company. Take me. I been with Hatch and Hodges for eight years; since I was a sixteen-year-old boy."

Then what?

"Yes, sir. I like it very much. See, my father is general manager up to Prescott. He said, 'Steve, if you're going to work for me you're going to start at the bottom and pull your ownself up.' Which is what I did—starting as a stable boy in the Prescott yard."

He thought: He's not interested in that.

But thought then: You got to talk, don't you? You have to be friendly.

"Then I went out, Mr. Glennan. Went to work for Mr. Rindo who's agent up on the Gila Ford to San Carlos run. Then my Uncle Joe Mauren, who isn't my uncle but that's what I call him, made me his shotgun messenger. Uncle Joe drove then. Now he's in charge of all construction. But when I was with him he taught me everything there is to know—how to drive, how to read sign, how to shoot. . . . But you met him! Mr. Mauren? The one first talked to you a couple weeks ago?"

See, he thought. You talk enough and it comes right back to where you started.

"So then I drove a stage for four years and then, just last week, was named a supervisor for the Bisbee to Contention section and for this new line that goes up to Rock of Ages. And that's why I'm the one calling on you with the franchise agreement."

See? Right back again.

You talk all your life and you don't worry about it, he thought. But when it's your job to talk then you worry like it's some new thing to learn. Like it's harder than hitting something with a Colt gun or driving a three-team stage.

★
Chapter Two

Two with Guns

A quarter of a mile ahead of Brady, two riders came down through the rocks and scrub brush to the mouth of the draw. They dismounted, leaving their horses in the trees, came out to the edge of the wagon ruts at the point where they entered the open meadow, and looked back up the draw.

The younger of the two, his hat low and straight over his eyes, and carrying a Henry rifle, said, "He'll be along directly." They moved back to the shadowed cover of the pine trees and stood there to wait.

"You don't know who he is," the second man said. "Why take a chance?"

"Where's the chance?" the younger man said. "If he moves funny I'll bust him."

"Ed wouldn't waste his time on one man."

"The hell with Ed."

"Ed looks for the big one."

"You don't know how big a thing is till you try it," the younger man said. He paused, raising the Henry carefully, pointing the barrel out through the pine branches. "There he is, Russ, look at him."

They watched Brady come out of the trees at the end of the draw and start across the meadow. For a moment the younger man studied him, his face relaxed but set in a tight-lipped grin. He said then, "He don't look like much. Maybe I'll skin him and take his hide."

"While you're talking to yourself, he's moving away," the other man said.

"All right, Russ, you're in such a big hurry." He raised the Henry to his shoulder and called out, "Hold it there!"

Brady reined in, half turning his mount.

"Don't look around!"

The younger man came out almost to the road, to the left of and slightly behind Brady. "Take your coat off, then the gun belt." Moving closer, keeping the Henry sighted on Brady's back, he watched Brady pull off the coat. "Now let it drop," he said.

"It'll get all dirty."

"Drop it!"

Brady obeyed, then unbuckled his gun belt and let it fall next to the coat.

"Now the Winchester."

Brady drew it from the saddle boot and lowered it stock down.

"You got business around here?"

"If I do it's mine," Brady answered. "Nobody else's."

He tried to turn, hearing the quick steps behind

him, but caught only a glimpse of the man before he was pulled off the saddle, and as he hit the ground and tried to roll away, the barrel of the Henry chopped against the side of his head to stop him.

The rifle barrel prodded him then. "Get up. That didn't hurt."

Brady pushed himself up slowly with a ringing in his ears and already a dull, hard pain in his temple. He felt the rifle barrel turn him to face the horse.

"Now stand like that while you take your shirt off and drop your pants."

"I can't go around without any clothes—" He felt the hand suddenly on his collar, pulling, choking him, then jerking and the shirt ripped open down the back. Behind him the man laughed.

"You don't know what you can do till you try," the man with the Henry said.

Brady pulled off the shirt without unbuttoning it, used his heels to work off his boots, let his pants drop then stepped into the boots again. He stood now in his long white underwear, wearing boots and hat, and staring at the smooth leather of his saddle close in front of him.

The second man came out of the trees. "Let him go now," he said.

"When I'm ready."

"You're ready now. Let him go."

"Russ, you're the nervous type." The Henry swung back on Brady—"Go on!"—then raised slightly as Brady stepped into the saddle, and the younger man said, "Don't he cut a fine figure, Russ?" He stood grinning, looking up at Brady, then moved toward him and yelled, "Kick him! Go on, *run*!"

As Brady started off, the man called Russ went back into the trees for the horses. When he came out, Brady was halfway across the meadow and the younger man was going through Brady's pockets.

"How much?" Russ asked.

"Ten dollars plus and some papers."

"What kind of papers?"

"How'd I know?"

"Bring them along, for Ed to look over."

"You can have them," the younger man said. He began unbuckling his gun belt and Russ frowned. "Where're you going?"

"Steppin' out, with my new suit on."

"Listen, you know what Ed said—"

"Russ, I don't care what old Ed thinks or says." He winked, grinning, kicking off his boots. "That's a fine-looking girl down there."

★ ★ ★

As JOE MAUREN had described it, the Glennan place was almost hidden in deep tree shadow: a stand of aspen bordering the front yard, pinyon close behind the house and beyond, on higher ground, there were tall ponderosa pines. The house was a one-story log structure with a shingle roof but an addition to it, built out from the side and back to form an L, was of adobe brick. A stable shed, also adobe and joined to the addition by twenty feet of fence, stood empty, its doors open.

Brady passed through the aspen, noticing the empty shed, then moved his gaze to the house, expecting the door to open, but thinking: Unless everybody's gone.

You're doing fine your first day.

Straight out from the door of the log house he reined in, waited a moment then started to dismount.

"Stay up!"

Over his shoulder Brady caught a glimpse of the girl standing at the corner of the house. She was holding a shotgun.

"You don't have to turn around, either!"

Brady shook his head faintly. He didn't move. Twice in one day.

The girl said, "You're a friend of Albie's, aren't you?"

"I never heard of him." Brady started to turn.

The shotgun barrel came up. "Keep your eyes straight!"

Brady shrugged. "I know what you look like anyway."

"Fine, then you don't have to be gawking around."

"Your head'd come up to about my nose," Brady said. "You look more boy than girl, but you got a pretty face with nice blond hair and dark eyes and eyebrows that don't match your hair."

"Albie told you that," the girl said. "You talk just like him."

"Miss Glennan, I'll take an oath I don't know any Albie." He cleared his throat before saying, "My name's Stephen J. Brady of the Hatch and Hodges Company come here to see your dad with the agreement—"

"You don't have any clothes on!"

Brady turned in the saddle to look at her and this time she said nothing to stop him. Her lips were parted and her eyes held him with open astonishment. He had time to take in details—the dark eyes that looked almost black, and her face and arms warm brown against the whiteness of her blouse and her hair that was pale yellow and combed back and tied with a black ribbon—seeing all this before the shotgun tightened on him again.

Brady said, "You've seen men's underwear before. What're you looking so shocked for?"

"Not with you in them," the girl said.

"I thought maybe I could borrow a pair of your brother's pants—"

"How'd you know I had a brother?"

"You got two. The little one, Mike, is in school down in Bisbee. The big one, Paul, whose pants I want to borrow till I get up to Rock of Ages and buy my own, is in the Army. Farrier Sergeant Paul J.

Glennan, with the Tenth down to Fort Huachuca."

The girl's eyes narrowed as she studied him. "You know a lot about my family."

"More'n Albie could've told me?"

The girl said nothing.

"I told you I was with Hatch and Hodges," Brady said. "A while back a man took my clothes, guns, and papers, and that's why I'm sitting here like this. But I can still prove I'm from Hatch and Hodges, and here to see your father."

"How?"

"All right," Brady said. "Your father's name is John Michael Glennan, born in Jackson, Michigan, in . . . 1837. Same town your mother's from. Your dad served with the late George Custer and was wounded in the Rock Creek fight at Gettysburg. Your brother Paul was born in '62. You came along in '65; then six years later your dad brought the family out here. You first settled up north near Cabezas, but there weren't enough trees there to suit him, so you came down here and been here ever since.

"Your dad's raised stock, but it never paid him much. Twice he wintered poorly and another year the market was down; so now he'd like to just raise horses and on the side, for steady money, run a stage line stop. Paul'll be out of the Army in six months; Mike out of school in a year. Your name's Catherine Mary Glennan and every word my Uncle Joe Mauren said about you is true."

"If it's a trick, it's a good one," the girl said. "You knowing all that."

"Sister, I'm trying to do my job, but I can't do it without my pants or my papers. Add to that your dad's not here anyway."

"How do you know that?"

"The stable door's open and your team and wagon's gone."

"They'll be back soon," the girl said quickly.

"Then I'll wait to talk to him."

"But I don't know when."

"You just said *soon*." Brady watched her. "Look, if you're worried about being alone with me I'll move along; but all I got to say is your dad must not want this franchise very much, else he'd be here."

"He *does* want it!" The girl moved toward him. "He had to drive my mother over near Laurel. There's a lady there about to deliver and Ma'd promised to help. But my dad said if you came, to explain it to you so there'd be no misunderstanding, because he does want to have that . . . whatever you call it."

"So you don't know when he'll be home."

"Probably tomorrow."

"Why didn't you tell me that before?" Brady said. " 'Stead of this business about he'll be back soon."

"Because I didn't know who you were," the girl said angrily. "In fact, I still don't. All I'm sure of is you're a man sitting there in your underwear and not much of a man at that to let somebody take your clothes right off you."

"He had a gun," Brady said.

"So did you!"

"But he had his first." Brady's hand went to the side of his face. "And he laid it across me early in the proceedings."

"Oh—"

"That's all right. Just leave me have the pants."

"And something to eat?" She was calm again and her eyes opened inquiringly. "You can ride around back, water your horse and yourself, and come in the back door."

"So the neighbors won't see me?" Brady said.

Chapter Three

Fine-Looking Girl

She smiled at him and after that—while she looked for her brother's pants; while Brady came out of the bedroom pulling up the faded green suspenders and asking her how he looked and she saying like a man who'd already been married twenty years; while they ate pancakes and drank coffee; while they just sat talking about everything in general and asking harmless-sounding questions about one another—they were at ease with each other and both seemed to enjoy it.

He explained how he had been robbed and told to ride on. How he had crossed the meadow then stopped, thinking about going back. But, one, it was good country to hide in; how would he find them? Two, even if he did, he had no gun. And three, which was part of two, they could even be laying for him, waiting to shoot him out of the saddle if he came back.

It was just poor luck, Brady said. But you had to expect so much of that in life; and if it happens the first day of a new job, maybe it's just the Almighty warning you not to be too cocky or full of yourself, else He'll whittle you down to size in one minute's time.

Catherine Mary said she'd never thought of that before, though she knew God moved in mysterious ways. Maybe He even sent Albie here as a warning, she said. A way of telling her to be cautious of the men she met until the right one came along. Albie was easy to see through. He smiled a lot and said nice things, but it was all on the surface.

And where had he come from? Two weeks ago, the first time he came by with another man. Her father was home and they'd stayed only long enough to water their horses, saying they were on their way to a job. Then a few days later, when just her mother and she were at the house, the younger one came back.

That was when he told his name and said he liked this part of the country very much and maybe he'd just stay around. But the way he looked at you and the sweet way he talked, you knew he was thinking something else. The third time he came, there wasn't any doubt about that.

She was alone in the stable when he walked in and right away started talking about how quiet and nice it was and wasn't she lonely never seeing a young man for weeks at a time? Then he tried to kiss her, so sure of himself that she almost had to laugh; but it wasn't funny when he put his arms around her and gave her one of those awful wet kisses. Then he let go and stepped back as if to say there, now you've been kissed you won't fight it anymore.

She didn't fight. She ran and got the shotgun and Albie rode out fast yelling back something about letting her cool off a while.

But what was he doing around here? That was the question. Where had he been living for the past two weeks?

Brady and the girl heard the horse at the same time and both looked at each other across the table, both taken by surprise and thinking no, it couldn't be. For a moment there was no sound. Then, "Kitty!"

She stood up quickly, looking at Brady. "It's him."

Brady said, "Boy, that's something, isn't it?" He was a few steps behind her going to the door, but close to her as she reached it raising the latch. He pulled the door open, stepping outside after her, and the first thing he saw was his new suit.

ALBIE WAS WEARING it. Albie glancing at the door-way as he swung his right leg over the horse, as the girl stepped out into the sunlight saying, "We were just talking about you." And as Albie's foot touched the ground and he started to turn, Brady reached him.

"But no need for talk now," Brady said. He saw the puzzled frown on Albie's face, his mouth slightly open and his eyes asking a question in the shadow of the curled, forward-tilted hat brim. His expression changed suddenly to recognition and at that moment Brady hit him, his right fist jerking up, slamming into the changing, tightening expression.

Albie stumbled against his horse, half turning to catch himself with both palms slapping against the saddle, but his horse side-stepped nervously and in the moment that Albie hung off balance Brady's left fist drove into his ribs, cocked again as his right hand pulled Albie around, then hooked solidly into his jaw. Albie stumbled back off balance and this

time he went down. He rolled to his side as he
struck the ground, his right hand going to his hip,
pulling back the coat, then hesitated.

Brady stood over him. "Try it, I'll stomp you
right into the ground."

Albie looked up, squinting and rubbing the side
of his jaw. "You her brother?"

"I got one thing to say to you," Brady answered.
"Take my suit off."

"If you're not a kin of hers," Albie said, "you
better be careful how you talk."

"Just take it off," Brady said.

He looked up, glancing again at the girl as she
called, "There's somebody coming."

He was aware of the faint hoofbeat sound then,
far off, but clear in the open stillness; and already
halfway across the meadow, coming toward them
from the pinyon slope that was perhaps four hundred yards away but seemed closer, he saw two riders. Directly behind them in the distance, the
wagon trail was a thin sand-colored line coming
down out of the dark mass of pinyon. They had de-
scended that road, Brady judged, the same way he
had come not an hour before.

Albie was on his elbow, turned now and watched
them approach. Brady saw the grin forming on his
mouth as they drew closer and again he glanced at
the girl. "Who are they?"

She stood motionless, one hand shading her eyes from the sun glare. A breeze moved the fullness of her skirt and her hand dropped to hold the bleached cotton material against her leg.

"I'm not sure," she answered.

"He knows them," Brady said.

She studied them intently before her expression changed. "Yes . . . the one on the left, he was with Albie the first time."

"Russ," Albie said, pushing himself up to a sitting position. "Russ is my ma and the other one's my pa." He laughed then and called out, "Hey, Ma, this boy's pickin' on me!" He came to one knee as the riders came out of the aspen stand, reining their horses to a walk.

The one called Russ, slouched easily in the saddle but with a Winchester across his lap said, "Albie, you're never going to learn."

Albie came to his feet, brushing the seat of his pants. He was grinning and said, "Learn what, Ma?"

"That boy's about to take his suit back."

"Like hell he is," Albie said.

Brady stepped toward him as he spoke and as Albie glanced around, Brady's left hand slammed into his face. Brady was on him as he went down, pressing his knee into his stomach, and when he rose he was holding the Colt Albie had been wearing. He saw that it was his own.

"I told you," Russ said.

Brady looked up at the two riders. "Either of you object?"

Russ shook his head. "Not us. It's your suit, I guess you can take it if you want."

"My Winchester, too," Brady said.

Chapter Four

Private Business

Russ hesitated. His right hand was through the lever and the barrel pointed just off from Brady. The second rider, who was bearded and wore a low-crowned, stiff-brimmed hat, held his hands one over the other on the saddle horn.

He said, "Russell, give Mr. Brady his piece." He spoke without straining to be heard and now his eyes moved from Brady—who was studying him curiously as he moved toward Russ to take the extended Winchester—to the girl and one hand lifted easily to touch his hat brim.

"You must be Kitty I've heard so much about." And as she nodded he said, "Has Albie been a botheration to you, Miss Glennan?"

"I have to tell you that he has," the girl said seriously. "And being his father, you should know about the things he's been doing—"

The bearded man's palm raised to interrupt her. "No, ma'am, I'll admit I took Albie in and treated him as blood kin, but there's no relationship between us." His eyes went to Brady then returned. "Ask Mr. Brady there, he'll tell you who I am. Though he knows me by a part of my life I've been struggling to forget."

Studying the bearded man, Brady frowned. "We've met before?"

"Bless your heart," the bearded man said. "It's a good feeling to know you can outlive the remembrance of past sins." He touched his hand to his hat brim again, looking at the girl. "My name is Edward Moak, ma'am, once a desperate outlaw, thieving and living off monies that were never rightfully mine, but never killing anybody you understand, until the day five years and five months ago I ran into this same Mr. Steve Brady and he ended my evil ways with one barrel-load of his scattergun." He looked at Brady. "Am I in the recollection of your past now, Mr. Brady?"

"On the Sweet-Mary to Globe run," Brady said, studying Edward Moak, picturing him as he had been: heavier, and with only a mustache. "You've changed some."

"Yuma will do that to a man," Edward Moak said.

"Cutting cell blocks out of solid rock will change a man physically, and it can cleanse him spiritually if he'll let it." His eyes went to the girl. "Which I did, Miss Glennan. I let it. The evil oozed out of my skin in honest labor and I felt newly baptized and born again in the bath of my own perspiration."

"Amen," Albie said. He was standing now. He had taken off Brady's coat and cartridge belt and now he stepped out of the pants and let them fall in the dust.

"You see," Moak said. "Albie's smart-alecky because he was raised in bad company and hasn't learned a sense of proper values. That's why I've taken up guiding him, so he'll profit by my experiences and not have to learn the Yuma way." Moak's eyes dropped to his hands on the saddle horn. "It's an easy road for some people, Miss Glennan; but others have to fight the devil every step of the way." He looked up then. "Say, are your folks here, Miss Glennan? Albie's told me about them and I'd be proud to make their acquaintance."

The girl shook her head. "They won't be back until tomorrow."

"That's a shame," Moak said. "Well, maybe some other time." He looked at Brady then. "I almost forgot, I still have something of yours." He stepped out of the saddle and walked around the two horses toward Brady, his legs moving swiftly in high boots. He wore a Colt on his right hip and as his hand moved to his inside coat pocket there was a glimpse of leather, a shoulder holster under his left arm. Brady saw it; but now his eyes were on Edward Moak's face, trying to read something there, but seeing only an easy grin in the short-trimmed beard.

"You've changed some yourself," Moak said. "Grown taller and filled out. You know I didn't get much of a look at you at the holdup." His grin broadened. "All I saw was that scattergun swingin' on me and then my whole left arm hurting like fire and next thing I was on the ground."

HE HELD THE ARM up stiffly. "Can only bend her about six inches, but I say that's little enough to pay for learning the way of righteousness.

"But I got a good look at you at the trial," Moak went on. "Remember, we were on facing sides of those two tables, only you on the right side and me on the wrong. Yes, sir, I got a good look at you that day. Heard you testify, heard you swear your name to be Stephen J. Brady—Then, not an hour ago, Russell hands me a billfold taken out of the wildness of Albie's youth, and the first thing I see when I open it is the name Stephen J. Brady." Moak shook his head. "I swear for all the country it's a small damn world."

"So it was in your mind to return the billfold," Brady prompted.

"To right a wrong," Moak agreed solemnly. "Though I didn't suspect I'd find you this easy. I figured to pick up young Albie here then go on toward Rock of Ages on the hunch you'd gone that way."

"Just a hunch?" asked Brady.

"Well," said Moak, "I couldn't help reading in your billfold you're a line superintendent—which is a fine thing going from shotgun messenger to line super in just five years and five months—so I felt you'd go there, Rock of Ages being your closest station." Moak paused. "You were, weren't you?"

"In time," Brady said.

"You're staying here a while?"

"I think so."

"You could ride with us," Moak said, "seeing we're both going the same way."

Their eyes held as they spoke. Brady was thinking, feeling the Colt in his right hand and the Winchester in his left pointed to the ground but with his finger through the trigger guards: *Watch him. Keep watching him.* And he said, "No, you go on. I haven't made plans yet."

"We'll be glad to wait on you, Mr. Brady," Moak said softly.

"You must have plenty of spare time," Brady said.

The grin showed in Moak's beard. "We're waiting on a business deal to go through."

"Damned if we aren't," said Albie. He was smiling, standing in his long underwear with hands on
thin hips, and he winked at Moak as the bearded
man glanced stern-faced at him.

Brady caught it. He said then, "I have private
business here with Miss Glennan, so you all go on."

Moak's eyebrows raised. "Now why didn't you
say that before? Sure we will." He turned to his
horse, motioning Albie to his, then took his time
stepping into the saddle. As he neck-reined to turn
he said, "Mr. Brady, I'm looking forward to seeing
you again."

He rode away, past the front of the house, along
the edge of the dense pines with Russell catching up
to him then, Albie following and looking back as
they neared the far point of trees. Brady and the
girl watched them all the way as they followed the
curve of the valley north.

As they rounded the edge of trees and passed
from sight the girl said, "He was lying, wasn't he?"

Brady looked at her. "How do you know?"

"Just the way he talked. And the little things,"
the girl said. "His friends, his two guns."

"You didn't miss anything."

"The way he kept staring at you."

"Like in the courtroom," Brady said.

"I'll bet he was mean that day."

"Swore to hunt me and kill me," Brady said. "Which you didn't hear him mention today. He carried on so, screaming and trying to get at me, it took four deputies to take him out."

"That was before he was born again," the girl said.

"Yeah," Brady said, "before he sweated out the badness."

They smiled at the same time and the girl said, "It's not funny, but it's kind of, isn't it?"

"That part is," Brady said. "But I'll bet what he's doing around here isn't funny." He watched the girl go over to his suit and pick it up, shaking out the dust. He watched her fold it over her arm as her eyes met his again.

"We could have some coffee," she said, "and talk about it."

Chapter Five

So They'll Be Back

They moved the table to the front window and sat next to each other facing it with the Winchester propped against the table edge.

Brady told her about the attempted stage holdup five years ago: how he had shot Ed Moak and how his Uncle Joe Mauren had gotten another man who lived only a few hours with a .45 bullet inside him. He told her what he knew about Ed Moak, things that were brought out at the trial and things he learned about him afterward: That he'd been an outlaw and a gunslinger as far back as anyone knew anything about him; had killed six men for sure, though some put it as high as ten. That he had a reputation for talking mildly and smiling when he talked, and everybody agreed that if a man wore two guns and no badge and did that, you'd better look out for him.

The girl said, So we take for granted he hasn't been reborn. And Brady said, Without even having to mention it.

There was only one reason Ed Moak would be here, would have stayed around for over two weeks, Brady concluded. Because money shipments took this road up to the Rock of Ages mine to meet the once-a-month payroll. There couldn't be any other reason and Moak almost admitted it himself when he said, "We're waiting on a business deal to go through," and Albie laughed and said something. By that time Moak must have been sure of himself and he wasn't so worried about us wondering what he was doing here.

You see, Brady explained, before that he didn't know who was around and he was slick, careful as could be. But then he made you tell that your father was gone till tomorrow and right after that he started to change, not too much, but as if it really didn't matter what we believed anymore. He was sure then that at least somebody he couldn't see wasn't aiming a gun at him.

And he might have made a play then, but by that time I was on guard, holding a Colt and a Winchester and he knew I'd use them—with a stiff left arm to testify to the fact.

So they made the show of riding away. It didn't have to be done then and there, face to face, not when they know they got all night.

The girl asked, "But why wouldn't they just leave for good?"

"With the odds in their favor?"

"But they wouldn't dare plan a holdup now. They're *known*."

"Only by us," Brady said.

"We're still enough to testify against them," the girl said earnestly. "They know that much."

She remembered being frightened in front of Edward Moak, then amused, considering it an unusual experience, one that would make good telling, especially if you described it almost casually. And for a moment she had even pictured herself doing this. But now, realizing it and not wanting to realize it, looking at Brady's face and waiting for him to say something that would relieve the nervous feeling tightening in her stomach, she knew that it was not over.

"Moak must have a good plan," Brady said, "to stay around here studying the land for two weeks. He's not going to waste it because of one man. Especially if the man's the same one almost shot his arm off one time. Then there's Albie. His pride's hurt and the only way to heal it is to bust me. So they'll be back."

The girl's eyes were open wide watching him. "And we just wait for them?"

"I've thought it out," Brady said. "First, I can't leave you here alone. As you said, you know their names. But two of us running for it would be hard put, not knowing where they are."

"You're saying you could make it alone," the girl said. "But I'd slow you down."

Brady nodded. "I'll say it's likely, but we'll never know because I'm not about to leave you alone."

"Mr. Brady, I'm scared. I don't know what I'd do if you left."

"I said I wouldn't. Listen, we're staying right here and that narrows down the possibilities. If they want us they'll have to come in here and they'll have to do it before tomorrow morning . . . before your dad's due back or anybody else who might happen along. Like my Uncle Joe Mauren."

The girl was silent for a moment. "But if they don't see you ride out they'll think you're . . . spending the night."

Brady smiled. "All right, you worry about our

good names and I'll worry about our necks. If Ed Moak believes that, that's fine. He'd think we don't suspect he's still around and he might tend to be careless."

Her eyes, still on his face, were open wide and she bit at her lower lip nervously thinking over his words.

"You're awful calm about it," she said finally.

"Maybe on the outside," Brady answered.

HE LEFT THE HOUSE twice that afternoon. The first time out the front door and around to the back, taking his time while his eyes studied the trees that began to close in less than a hundred feet away, just beyond the barn and the smaller outbuildings. He took his horse to the barn before returning to the house.

Less than forty feet away, directly he went to the barn, counting eighteen steps diagonally to the right from the house to the barn door. He milked the single cow in the barn, fed the horses—three, counting his own—checked the rear door which had no lock on it, then took the grain bucket he had used and propped it against the front door with a short-handled shovel. He picked up the milk pail and went out, squeezing past the door that was open little more than a foot.

His eyes went to the back of the stable that was directly across from the barn then along the fence to the house. He walked to the right, passed a corn crib that showed no corn in it through the slats, then turned to the house and went inside, bolting the back door.

They waited and now there was little to talk about. He told her one of them might try sneaking up through the barn to get their horses; but there wasn't much they could do about that. He told her about propping the grain bucket against the door and what he would do and what she would do if they heard it fall. Maybe they wouldn't hear it though. There were a lot of maybe's and he told her the best thing to do was not even think about it and just wait.

"Maybe they've gone and won't come," the girl said.

"That's right, maybe they've gone and won't even come."

Though neither of them believed that.

They watched the darkness creep in long shadows down out of the trees and across the meadow. It came dingy and dark gray over the yard bringing with it a deep silence and only occasional night sounds. When the room was dim the girl rose and brought a lamp to the table, but Brady shook his head and she sat down again without lighting it.

Now neither of them spoke and after a time Brady's hand moved to hers on the table. His fingers touched her fingers lightly. His hand covered hers and held it. They sat this way for a long time,

at first self-consciously aware of their hands together, then gradually relaxing, still not speaking,
but feeling the nearness of one another and experi-
encing in the touch of their hands a strange warm
intimate feeling, as if they had known each other
for years and not just hours.

They sat this way as Brady's fingers moved and
rubbed the back of her hand lightly, feeling the
small bones and the smoothness of her skin, and
when her hand turned their palms came together
and held firmly. They sat this way until the faraway
sound of a falling bucket clanged abruptly out of
the darkness.

Brady came to his feet. He heard the girl gasp
and he said, "Hold on to yourself. Remember now,
you stay in here. You don't open the door unless
you hear my voice."

He went out the front door, closing it quietly,
now moving along the front of the house. At the
corner he drew his Colt, eased back the hammer,
hesitated only a brief moment before crouching and
running along the fence to the front of the stable.
He stopped to listen, then moved again, around the
stable and along its adobe side to the back corner
and now he went down to one knee.

Less than forty feet away directly across from
him, the door of the barn came slowly open. Someone hesitated in the black square of the opening before coming out cautiously, keeping close to the

front of the barn until he reached the corner. Brady waited, his eyes going from the dark figure to the open doorway, but no one followed.

You know who it is, Brady thought, raising, aiming the Colt. You know blame well who it is. He's alone because he ran out of patience. Too young and full of fire to sit and wait. All right. That's fine. Albie, you're digging your own hole and that's just fine.

He watched the figure leave the barn: sidestepping cautiously out of the deep shadow, facing the house with his drawn gun, but edging one step at a time toward the dim outline of the corn crib.

Don't give him a chance, Brady thought. But as his hand tightened on the trigger he called out, "Albie—"

Albie fired. There was no hesitation, no indecision. With the sound of his name, his gun hand swung across his body and fired and with the movement he was running, going down as he reached the corn crib.

Silence.

So you learn, Brady thought. But you don't make the same mistake twice. He stepped out past the corner of the stable bringing up the Colt and lining the barrel on the empty corn crib.

Three times in quick succession he aimed and fired, moving the Colt from right to left across the shape of the crib. The sounds clashed in the darkness: the heavy ring of the Colt, the ripping, whining of the bullets splintering the slats and with the third shot a howl of pain.

Brady moved quickly across the yard to the corner of the barn. He loaded the Colt, listening, watching the crib, then edged around the corner, dropped to his hands and knees and crept toward the crib. Albie was on his knees doubled over holding his arms tight to his stomach when Brady pressed the Colt into his back.

"Get up, Albie."

"I can't move." The words came out in short grunts.

"You're going to move one more time," Brady said. He took Albie's gun then went quickly across to the house and called the girl's name. The door opened and he saw the relief in her eyes and saw her about to speak, but he said, "Albie's not going to last."

"Oh—" He saw her bite her lower lip.

"Listen—but maybe we can still use him." Brady spoke hurriedly, but quietly, telling her what to do: to hold Albie's gun on him and not move it even though he was doubled over with a bullet through his middle. And after that Brady ran to the barn. He went through it seeing only the cow, then out the rear door and across the wagon ruts into the trees. A dozen yards back in the pines he found their horses picketed with Albie's. He led them back to the barn and came out the front leading only Albie's.

The girl's eyes were open wide. "He's hurt terribly bad."

Brady said nothing. Albie screamed as Brady

stooped and pulled him to his feet and made him mount the horse. Brady said then, "Listen to me. We're giving you a chance. Go get some help. You hear me, go get Ed to take care of you." He slapped the horse's rump, jumped after it and slapped again and the horse broke into a gallop—with Albie doubled over, his hands gripping the saddle horn—and rounded the corner of the stable.

Taking the girl's hand, Brady led her through the house, opened the front door then stood in the doorway, his hand holding her arm.

"I don't understand," she said.

"Listen a minute." They could still hear Albie's horse, though faintly now in the distance. "Going straight across," Brady said. "Telling us where Mr. Moak's waiting."

Chapter Six

Two to One Odds

Now think about it some more, Brady thought. He was by the window again staring out at the masked, unmoving shapes in the darkness and hearing the small sounds of the girl who was in the kitchen, beyond the blanket that draped the door-

way. Kitty. No—Catherine Mary. Brady said
Catherine Mary again to himself, listening to the
sound of it in his mind.

All right, and what're the odds on calling her
that tomorrow?

Two to one now. Getting better. But now what will
they do? You know what you'll do, but what about
them? Was Albie on his own? Maybe. Or part of a
plan. Maybe. One of them is back in the trees and the
other one's in front, across the meadow. Maybe.
Could you run for it now, both of you? Maybe. Or
will Ed Moak run for it? Hell no. One, two, three,
four maybe's and a hell no—so the changing of the
odds doesn't change your situation any. You still sit
and wait. But now he knows you're not asleep.

He moved around the table to the side of the window and looked diagonally out across the yard.
The aspen stand showed ghostly gray lines and a
mass of branches and beyond it, in the smoked
light of part of a moon, the meadow was mist gray
and had no end as it stretched to nothing.

"Will he die?" the girl asked. She had made no
sound coming to stand close to him.

"I think he will," Brady said. The girl did not
speak and he said then, "I didn't want to kill him. I
wanted to shoot him. I mean I was trying to shoot
him because I had to, but killing him or seeing him
dead wasn't in my mind."

His eyes moved to her face. She was staring out

at the night and Brady said, "You feel sorry for him now."

"I can't help it." Her voice was low and with little tone.

"Listen, I felt sorry for him when I put him on the horse. He was just a poor kid going to die and I didn't like it one bit—but all the time I kept thinking, we're still in it. There's no time out for burying the dead and saying Our Fathers because Ed Moak is still here and knowing it is the only thing in the whole world that's important."

"Unless he's gone," the girl said.

"I just finished adding up the maybe's," Brady said. "You want to know how many there are?"

"I'm sorry."

"No, I shouldn't have said that."

She turned to him. "You remind me a lot of my older brother."

"I hope that's good."

She smiled. "I believe everybody likes Paul. He's never put on or anything."

"Yeah?" There was a silence before Brady said, "You know, I was thinking, you haven't once cried or carried on or—you know, like you'd think a girl would."

"All girls don't act like that."

"I guess not." Brady said then, "You can learn a lot in a few hours, can't you?"

"Things that might've taken months," the girl said.

"Or years."

"It's funny, isn't it?"

"It's strange—"

"That's what I mean."

Brady said, "I've been thinking about you more than about Ed Moak."

HER FACE WAS CLOSE to his, but now she looked out the window not knowing what to say.

"I didn't have any trouble telling you that," Brady said. "Which is something, for me."

She looked at him again, her face upturned calmly now and again close to his. "What is it you're telling me, Mr. Brady?"

"You know."

"I want to hear it."

"It would sound funny."

"That's all right."

He leaned closer and kissed her, holding her face gently between his hands. He kissed her again, hearing the soft sound of it and feeling the clinging response of her lips. His hands dropped to her waist as her arms went up and around his neck and they remained this way even after they had kissed, after his lips had brushed her cheek and whispered close to her ear.

"See?"

"It didn't sound funny."

"What's your ma and dad going to say?"

"They'll say it's awful sudden."

"Will they object?"

"Mr. Brady, are you proposing?"

He smiled, leaning back to look at her. "That's what you call the natural thing, when you're proposing and don't even know you're doing it."

"Then you are."

"I guess so."

"Can you be sure," she said seriously, "knowing a person just a few hours?"

"We could wait if you want. Say about a week."

"Now you're fooling."

"Not very much."

Catherine Mary smiled now. "I think this has been the fastest moving day of my life."

"But the longest," Brady said. "And it's not even over yet." He saw her smile fade and again he remembered Ed Moak and the other man; he pictured them in the darkness, waiting and not speaking.

He thought angrily: Why does he have to be here? Why should a man who you've seen once before in your life have a chance to ruin your life? He felt restless and suddenly anxious for Moak to come. He wanted this over with; but he made himself think about it calmly because there was nothing he could do but wait.

ALL NIGHT HE remained at the window, occasionally rising, stretching, moving about when the restlessness would return, though most of the time he sat at the table staring out at the darkness, now and again turning to look at the girl who was asleep, covered with a blanket and curled in a canvas-bottomed chair she had moved close to the table. (He had told her to go to bed, but she argued that she wouldn't be able to sleep and she sat in the canvas chair as a compromise. After some time she fell asleep.) Brady waited and the hours dragged.

But to the girl, the night was over suddenly. Something awakened her. She opened her eyes, saw Brady bending over her, felt his hand on her shoulder and beyond him saw the tabletop and the window glistening coldly in the early morning sunlight.

His expression was calm, though grave and quietly determined and when he spoke his words brought her up in the chair and instantly awake.

"They're coming now," Brady said.

"Where?"

"From across. Riding over like it's a social call." He watched her as she leaned close to the table, looking out and seeing them already approaching the aspen stand. "Catherine Mary, I want you to stay inside with the shotgun."

"What're you going to do?"

"Listen to me now—hold the shotgun on Russell. Then I won't have to worry about him." He hesitated uncertainly. "Are you afraid to use it?"

"No—"

"All right, and the Winchester's here on the table."

Facing the window he felt her hand on his arm, but now he moved to the door, not looking at her, and stepped outside before she could say anything more. He watched them coming through the aspen stand, walking their horses into the yard where, perhaps thirty feet from Brady, they stopped.

"Well, you sure must've had plenty of business," Ed Moak said easily. He swung down and still holding the reins a few steps ahead of his horse. "We didn't figure to see you still here."

Moak's words came unexpectedly, catching Brady off guard. He had pictured the bearded man calling bluntly for a fight; but this was something else. "It got late," Brady said. "I thought I might as well stay here."

"I can't say's I blame you," Moak said.

"What do you mean by that?"

Moak shrugged, almost smiling. "Not important. What we came for was to ask if you've seen young Albie hereabouts."

Talk to him, Brady thought hesitantly, in this one moment trying to see through Moak's intention; and said, "Haven't seen him."

"He rode out last night not saying for where and never come back."

"I can't help you," Brady said.

"Maybe Miss Glennan saw him."

"She would've said something about it."

"I suppose." Moak shifted his weight from one foot to the other. Standing in front of his horse the reins were over his left shoulder and pulled down in front of him with both hands hanging on the leather straps idly just above his belt line. His coat was open.

When you least expect it, Brady was thinking. That's when it'll come. His hands felt awkwardly heavy and he wanted to do something with them, but he let them hang, picturing now in his mind his right hand coming up with the Colt, cocking it, firing it. Then swinging it on Russell. Aim, he thought. You have to take your time. You have to hurry and take your time.

Moak shifted his feet again. "Russell, we might as well go on." The mounted man said nothing, but he nodded, glancing from Brady to Moak. "What about it?" Moak said to Brady again. "Does it suit your complexion to ride with us?"

"I've business with Mr. Glennan," Brady said. "He's coming along directly."

Moak grinned, glancing at Russell again. "Brady still don't want our company. . . . Well, we'll have to just go on without him."

Now, Brady thought.

He watched Moak turn, looping the right rein over the horse's head. He moved to the saddle, his left hand holding the reins and now reaching for the saddle horn. He stood close to the horse, about to step into the stirrup. And then was turning, pushing away the saddle as his right hand came out of his coat—

And as he had practiced it in his mind Brady drew the Colt, thumbed the hammer, brought it to arm's length, saw the shocked surprise of Moak's face over the front sight, saw the flash of metal in his hand, saw him falling away as the metal came up, shifted the front sight inches, all this in one deliberate nerve-straining motion—and pulled the trigger.

Russell saw the Colt pointed at him then. He shook his head. "Not me, sonny, this was just Ed's do." He dismounted and the Colt followed him to where Moak lay sprawled on his back.

"You can still see the surprise," Russell said. "He's dead, but he still don't believe it." He looked at Brady then. "I warned him. I said you'd be ready and wouldn't get caught on one foot. But all night long he sat rubbing his bad arm and saying what he was going to do to you. Said you'd break up in little pieces with the wait and he'd get you when the right time came.

"Then Albie stole off and come back dead in his saddle. Ed didn't talk for a while. Then he said how he'd ride in at daylight like we didn't know anything about Albie and take you by surprise. I told him again you'd be wide awake, but he wouldn't listen and now he's lying there."

Brady said, "You were planning to hold up a mine payroll, weren't you?"

"You can't prove anything like that," Russell answered.

"Well, it doesn't matter now anyway."

"Listen, I wasn't with him on this. You can't prove that either."

"No, now you're on our side, now it's over."

"I'm not on anybody's side."

"All right, just get out of here."

"We'll bury him first," Russell said. "Back in the trees there."

"I'm telling you to get out! Take him and get out of here right now—you hear me!"

Russell stared at him, then shrugged and said, "All right," quietly. He lifted Moak's body, straining, pushing him belly-down up over the saddle; then looked at Brady again and said, "Why don't you go buy yourself a drink."

"I'm all right."

"Sure you are. But it wouldn't do no harm."

Russell mounted and rode out of the yard leading Moak's horse.

Brady watched them until they were out of sight. He closed his eyes and he could still see Moak's legs hanging stiffly and his arms swinging and bouncing with the slow jogging motion of the horse—and he thought: God have mercy on him. And on Albie.

He holstered the Colt then raised his arm and rubbed his sleeve over his forehead, feeling tired and sweaty and feeling a fullness in his stomach that made him swallow and swallow again. And God help *me,* he thought.

He heard the girl behind him before he turned and saw her—not smiling, but looking at him seriously, with her lips parted, almost frowning, her gaze worried and not moving from his face.

"Are you all right?"

"I guess so."

Looking at the girl he knew that if he wasn't all right now, at least he would be. In time.

The stories contained in this volume originally appeared in the following publications:

"Apache Medicine," *Dime Western Magazine*, May 1952

"Red Hell Hits Canyon Diablo," *10 Story Western Magazine*, October 1952

"The Last Shot," *Fifteen Western Tales*, September 1953

"Blood Money," *Western Story Magazine*, October 1953

"Saint with a Six-Gun," *Argosy*, October 1954

"Man with the Iron Arm," *Complete Western Books*, September 1956

"The Longest Day of His Life," *Western Novel and Short Stories*, October 1956